THE HOUSE ON POULTNEY ROAD

A True Ghost Story

BY

STEPHANIE BODDY

PUBLISHED BY SCAMPS Publishing

978-0-9928092-0-1

Acknowledgements

I would like to take this opportunity to thank my family, friends and to all those involved in the making of this book. For sharing your stories that have scared but yet fascinated me for so many years (yes Richie, I'm talking to you!) To my husband for his tremendous support even though he still struggles to believe the content; and to my Mum, the sexy siren, who is my rock in all I do.

I'd also like to thank those who are no longer with us but who I know are in spirit. To the Granddad I never met, thank you for giving me the belief, aspiration, storyline and enthusiasm to write my first novel.

Chapter One

The same as most other years, the house on Poultney Road was up for sale. I grabbed the opportunity to view the house I'd heard so much about. I was desperate to be able to sift reality from the fictional image I'd created in my mind. Not wanting to go alone, and with my parents being away, I talked my disbelieving boyfriend, Elliott, into coming with me. We'd been together two years and, although we are best friends and bear no secrets, the house on Poultney Road was not something we had discussed in any great depth.

The house is only thirty minutes from where I lived with my parents and the ride there was smooth. The weather was particularly warm for June and the fact that our motorway journey was surrounded by blue skies and green fields, made me feel slightly less anxious.

"I don't want to go in." Elliott said, mocking me; his piercing brown eyes absorbing my reaction.

Elliott is a sceptic. He has little faith in God and even less in the afterlife. I've wasted no time in telling him about my family's history, about what had taken over their lives for so many years. Not that he would disbelieve me or my family but I know he would find it hard to accept what they had been a part of.

"You can wait in the car if you really want to but it's going to be hard enough trying to convince the current owners that such a young couple has £450k to spend on a house let alone a single woman," I replied sternly. My expression softening, I continued, "please, I need you to support me with this."

I watched as a smile appeared on Elliott's' face. "Of course I'm coming in with you, can't wait to meet some ghosts!"

When we arrived, we parked in a space directly outside the house. I sat for a moment and looked up at the very grand but tired-looking building. The bricks were now discoloured, far from the blood red colour they had once been, and I could see that they were crumbling around the edges. I tried to envision beyond the exterior, the tatty blinds and grubby seals, and worked hard to imagine number 106 Poultney Road as my family had almost a century ago. The display of crumbling bricks and markedly worn woodwork in front of me, was once a charming, inviting home. As hard as I fought with the image in front of me, I was unable to do it; this house could never be inviting. Although it appeared nothing out of the ordinary and quite similar to the houses which surrounded it, number 106 stood alone.

The second floor had two large windows at the front of the house, which was north facing, and I could imagine it being very dark and dismal inside, so the more windows meant maximum light getting in. There was one small, square window which sat above the front door, and a larger window which replicated the one beneath it. A small window sat on the third floor, and looked as though it was the gateway to an attic or converted loft space. It looked quite dark and not very inviting. I would be giving that floor a miss.

More than a century old, this house, Florence Villa, was erected in honour of Colonel Pulteney Henry Murray in 1882. A captain during the Egyptian War, the house should stand tall and represent a great man who fought for our country. It seems that, ironically, although the house was built as a mark of respect to a man who served during the war, and has withstood two world wars since then, it now has to face a continuous battle of its own. I suppose that when it was erected all those years ago, never did anyone imagine that such devastation and horror would be wrecked.

We made our way up the front steps and stood in front of the rather underwhelming, crimson-coloured front door. To the right of it was a large, rectangular window which hid thick, cigarette-tarnished net behind it.

"I don't want to go in. What happens if a ghost jumps out and scares me," Elliott mocked.

"Shut up and keep comments like that to yourself, or at least keep them quiet until we leave." I answered, unimpressed by his humour.

I think spirits and the afterlife have been so commercialised over the years that society has come to the conclusion that because it doesn't see the dead walking down the street or have spirits asking for help, that those who do experience any paranormal activity, or mediums as some people like to refer to them, are regarded as fakes.

Elliott, as I previously said, does not believe in the paranormal nor understand those who do.

We knocked on the door and waited to be greeted. I'm not sure how I felt. A combination of anxiety, fear, apprehension? I felt like I had already grown accustomed to the inside of the house because of the many stories I had been told growing up. Although I had never been inside, I felt like this house was as much part of my childhood as was my family's. It was a strange feeling when, in fact, I had no idea what was beyond the grand, red front door.

"Come in. Come in." Mrs Robinson was a well-spoken woman, perhaps recently reaching her fortieth birthday. Much taller than me, with dirty blond locks, she extended her wafer-like hand to greet me. "Have you come far?"

I could smell an underlying stench of cigarettes on her breath which usually wouldn't concern me quite as much as it did that summer evening. It almost made me retch.

"No, not really," I replied, continuing, "Have you had much interest in the property? How long has it been on the market?"

Besides her bad breath, I noticed that Mrs Robinson paused before she replied, "Since March; just two months. We've had a few people view the house but the train station at the back seems to put most of them off. I've recently asked for the ad to be more specific about the location of the property so that people come prepared. Did you see that the house was next to the station?" she asked.

"Yes," I replied, "I saw it in the description."

Already aware of the location of this property, I've always thought that this contributes to the house being even more susceptible to 'passing traffic'. Thousands of commuters fleet past every day, the house can sense life and thrives on its energy.

It was hard to believe that I was standing where it all started, so many years ago. A building which nurtured and matured several generations of my family; number 106 Poultney Road wasn't your typical haunted house. It wasn't isolated or miles from society but instead situated in a busy street next to a hectic train station used every day, every minute by commuters. As I stepped inside, it wasn't what I expected; in fact, I was disappointed. It was an anti-climax. For so many years I'd created an image in my mind of how this house should look, it's layout, decor, lighting; everything pictured perfectly in my mind to match the many stories I'd collected. Instead it felt like a grand building of emptiness.

I was immediately aware of how dark it was and how much bigger it was than what I'd expected from the online directory or even from standing outside. To my right was the front room, into which we were led.

"This is the TV room. Excuse my son, he's back from university and seems to have   taken over the house."

I looked about the room. Everything appeared to be normal of that of a house more than a hundred years old. It had traditional high ceilings and a gorgeous stone fireplace which I presumed was an original feature. Her son was laid out on the brown leather sofa with his eyes glued to the television. He looked about sixteen with greasy black hair, and oily skin to match. I found it hard to believe he was old enough to be at university but it was none of my business, so didn't utter a comment. He grunted something under his breath which I guessed was some kind of greeting but I wasn't sure so didn't reply.

"So how long have you lived here?" I enquired whilst returning myself to the tour.

"Almost five years," she replied, slightly hesitant, "on and off. My husband and I own a house in Switzerland and spend most of our time there. In fact, we have tried to sell this house on several occasions but I think because of the current climate, people are choosing cheaper locations away from the city or renovating what they already own."

I nodded as though I agreed with her but I knew that the recession wasn't the problem or the reason why the house was always up for sale. Although I joined in with her small talk, I never lost sight of my purpose. What I found particularly strange was the lack of atmosphere the house had. Although I was not unaccompanied and there were, with limits, furnishings around me, I felt alone.

We moved from the TV room back to the hallway. The dark walls that surrounded me were so obscure that you could only imagine the secrets they were hiding. We walked past a door leading under the stairs. I continued on as I felt I would have been prying to ask to look in there, but I tried to recall whether or not my family had mentioned a basement.

"This was previously my husband's study, it's the perfect size." Mrs Robinson gestured towards a room that sat at the back of the house next to the lounge. "It would also be an ideal playroom," Mrs Robinson threw a discreet but yet inappropriate smile in my direction.

The room was empty, the walls painted in mint green which reminded me of my parents' second sitting room at home. I had fond memories there and this translated through the paint, I felt calm walking in. I had to agree that it would make an ideal office and probably not a bad size for a playroom should Elliott and I have been planning children, or even had an intention of buying the property.

At the ripening age of twenty-seven, I was often complimented by people saying how young I looked and frequently asked for ID when buying alcohol. Although sometimes frustrating, particularly when, in a failed attempt to produce my ID that I'd left it at home, I always took it as a compliment. I think it's due to my petite frame. I'm not beautiful, I simply try to make the best of what God dealt me and, for Elliott, it seemed to do nicely.

I guess that Mrs Robinson imagined the house to be the first home Elliott and I would cohabit, not knowing that we already shared a perfect little home in the country, miles from the city; somewhere cocooned from the busy, dirty streets and bustling stations of London. Even if I had that lottery win, I wouldn't ever consider the house on Poultney Road.

"The garden's a nice size", I said, changing the subject and attempting to encourage more prospective house-viewing conversation. Looking out of the glass back door I added, "Is it south facing?"

"It is and although you can probably hear the trains pulling into the station, the fence stands high enough that people can't see into the garden and the noise becomes second nature after no time. We hardly know the station's there anymore."

This wasn't true; she was lying to get a sale. On several occasions my mother and I, climbed onto the brim attached to the metal fence on the side of the train platform and peered into the garden. Mum would often revive the story of how it was my Granddad Dick who built the conservatory on the back of the house. As for the growl of the passing train, I think that this would be the least of the prospective new tenants' problems.

We moved out of the study room and into the kitchen which overlooked the garden and railway line. Prior to viewing the property, my Mum and Dad had described the back of the house as being very tight and dark. Musky. Yet as I walked into this room, it felt quite the opposite. Very bright, modern and, in my opinion, the feature of the house, and making the rest of downstairs look very drab and in need of a revamp. The light, ceramic floor and egg-shell walls felt welcoming. Almost.

"The floor's heated?" Having politely left his shoes at the front door, Elliott could feel the warmth under his feet contrasting against the bitter cold around him.

"Yes, we built this room with every necessity and accessory in mind. We wanted this to be the room we bring friends into and spend most of our time as a family. This is my favourite room of the house. We decorated it, or should I say, gutted and rebuilt it about two years ago, before that it was honestly quite nasty."

I looked around at the wall mounted clock and read the words, HOME SWEET HOME displayed across it. I wondered if they wished they'd chosen a less ironic catchphrase. The kitchen was filled with top of the range accessories, a Range cooker, dainty gingham blinds and gorgeous white quartz tiles. I was intrigued as to how exactly the room was laid out before the transformation so that I could see everything I had in my head come to life before me. I asked,

"How much has it changed? Sorry to pry but I'm eager to know how such a gorgeous room could have ever looked anything but."

Elliott threw me a look. I knew this look well. It was a similar look a parent would give a child that was trying to cross a busy road without holding an adult's hand. A look of caution but, as ever, I couldn't help but be curious and stepped out without looking in either direction.

"Dramatically. It is now one large living space but it used to be three small rooms; three very dark rooms." Mrs Robinson trailed off into thought.

It was hard to imagine it any different to how it looked when we saw it. The large window on the back wall, overlooking the garden, brightened up an otherwise gloomy house. A window to the outside world, an escape.

The very tall, naturally blond, lady described how the room was once divided by thick walls. The first sitting area had a fireplace built into the far side and had just one narrow, murky window which let in very little light. The room was broken up by a door leading to a very small kitchen with worn out goods and broken work-tops. She explained how there was previously another, smaller, room at the very back of the house, and that the room was uncomfortable to be in.

"We never used the room, only to store things. It makes me cringe just at the thought of it."

I know of this room, I know that it was my Granddad who built it before he passed away. I desperately wanted to ask more, find out why she hated the room so much; why did it feel so depressing? But before I could think about being a little more inquisitive, Elliott and I were ushered out of the kitchen and back into the hall.

"Would you like to make your way upstairs?" Mrs Robinson asked.

"Before we do," I interrupted, "can I have a quick look at the garden?"

"Of course, the easiest way to get out would be to go back through the study."

As I made my way through the empty study, Elliott decided to stay back, not wearing his shoes he didn't want to go outside. As I pushed the door open, I was surprised by the size of the garden and the light it trapped. The house was so dark inside that it was hard to imagine such a bright, light absorbing exterior. I spotted two cats sitting on the wooden table.

"Ah, do these come as part of the furniture?" I joked.

"No, they hardly ever make their way indoors, only to eat. They tend not to like being inside, they prefer the fresh air."

I knew why. Animals are sensitive to any supernatural presence so I was sure that their senses would be doing over time inside number 106.

As I joined Elliott back inside, he took my hand. I think he knew I was feeling apprehensive about the rest of the tour.

"You can have a look around upstairs by yourselves if you would like. Get a feel for the place." Mrs Robinson insisted.

We made our way up the stairs and as we did, I took note of every detail. The bare cream walls were stained almost the entire height of the staircase. It looked as though furniture had been scraped and knocked around, taking the paint off the walls and leaving dents in its path.

"Just how Mum described it. Split staircase. Open hallway." As I recalled, I was trying to absorb every detail to relay to my Mum who, although desperate to come visit the place, was on a small Spanish Island enjoying the sunshine and sipping sangria.

"This must be my Lolly Nan and Great Granddad's bedroom, much smaller than I had pictured." I said quietly, tiptoeing my way across the landing and into the first bedroom down the long, thin corridor.

"Lolly Nan?" Elliott echoed, confused.

"My Great Nan used to spend every afternoon looking out onto the busy station road and wait for children to walk past on their route home from school. She would throw sweets out to them as they walked underneath the window. Lolly Nan was what every local knew her as."

Elliott remained silent, looking at me and allowing me to enjoy the story that had been shared with me so often. I have a selective memory. Bearing in mind I was just three years old when my Lolly Nan passed away, I can remember visiting her in hospital with my mum and taking jam donuts with us. I recollect sitting with her by an open window and giggling as she attempted to eat the jam donut without any teeth and getting more sugar and jam around her face than she managed to consume. Perhaps her love of sweets and her nickname were ironic and the cause of her tooth loss. I don't know for sure but what I do know is that memory will stay with me my whole life.

The room was small and dark, at the side of the house with very little light shining in. Although it looked dingy, it actually felt quite neutral; I would have felt comfortable staying there.

"I don't feel anything spooky happening. Do you?" Elliott whispered whilst creeping around the room, opening cupboards and generally being nosey. "I wonder why it seems no one lives here, it's like a hollow shell. It doesn't feel homely at all does it?"

I didn't answer as I could hear footsteps coming up the stairs. Not leaving us for long, Mrs Robinson joined us in the doorway.

"How do you like it? Have you seen the master bedroom yet? I love this room. It's the largest and brightest." Mrs Robinson led us from the small side room into a very bright and airy room at the front of the house.

The smell hit me instantly. Flowers? No; perfume, a sickly sweet fragrance. It was so strong, so dense that it felt as though it could be choking me. I stood as close to the door as I could. The room had character, unlike the rest of the house. It had the original fireplace, which I liked. The front wall was filled with a ceiling to floor window which, we were told, was a recent addition.

"Before we had these fitted there had been much smaller sash windows which seemed to swallow up the light," we were told.

I could see why they would want to improve the light quality. The window in this room seemed to be the only gateway to the outside world and the only source of natural light throughout the upper level.

"If you follow the hall to the back of the house you'll pass two bathrooms and come to the large spare room. I won't follow you; I'll let you explore the rest at your own pace. I'll be downstairs when you're done." Mrs Robinson could barely look us in the eye; an odd reaction for someone who was desperate to be selling their beloved family home.

There was only one bathroom, the other was just a toilet and basin. Both looked as though they were in dire need of a revamp or at least some bleach. It seemed to get colder the further into the house we went, whether this was due to the lack of sunlight I'm unsure, but a chill ran down my spine as we took the three steps down into what seemed to be an extension of the hallway. A low bookcase full of classic titles such as Jane Eyre and Wuthering Heights; a child's chair sat in the corner to the left of me. I wouldn't say that the furniture was ugly, just a little out of place in such an emotionless house, like keeping a dolly in a house with no children.

In front of us stood a solid wood door which was closed shut and shielding us from whatever miseries my parents had warned me about. This was the room that I'd heard so much about. The room which was once split in two, a sitting room and small kitchen like a self-contained flat which, years ago, my great-grandparents had made into their home. It was also the room that my five-year-old sister and three-year-old cousin used to refuse to go near, and would scream and have tantrums if they were taken anywhere close. The room to a hundred secrets stood so lonely in front of me.

The instant I walked into the back room, for the first time I felt the history of the house confined to a 10ft square space. A chill ran down my spine. If it were possible for a room to be vacuumed of air, then this would be my conclusion to the sudden intense density. I felt a bitter chill in strong contrast to the summer humidity outside. The interior was simple, lacking furniture as well as charm. Plain cream walls, covered in tears, black rubber marks and other dirty, mouldy looking stains with matching, vile carpet. To be honest it looked as though no one had been in the room for a while. Similar to other rooms in this outsized property, it felt unlived in. Although I wanted to spend as little time in there as possible, something drew me to the window. It was on the back wall, overlooking the garden and train station which seemed quiet, somewhat distant on that humid, dull day.

"Come on, let's go, they'll wonder what we are up to!" Grabbing me around my waist, Ell spoke with humour in his voice but it was wasted as even the sparkle in his eye went unnoticed as I pulled myself from his grip.

"Hang on, I just want to ...." My voice trailed off as my eyes searched the garden.

Everything appeared to be the same as when I stepped outside before; the green grass, neat marl grey and red patio. I witnessed the cats rapidly depart from their comfortable position on the wooden table as I was drawn to a sudden movement that came from the back of the garden, beside the small wooden shed in the left hand corner. As my eyes focused in on the movement, I realised that there was a figure flinching in the rear corner of the patio, I was positive that what I could see was a person. As it became clearer, it was evident that what I was seeing was indeed a child. With their back to me it was difficult to determine any features but, as my eyes adjusted, I could clearly see that it was a little girl, no more than five years old. Wearing a turquoise velvet dress, her long brown hair covered the top of the matching bolero jacket. Strangely I recognised the outfit; the colour, the beaded detail reminded me of a dress I once owned. I couldn't breathe, the air was filling my lungs as I lost the ability to inhale and exhale coherently, I realised that her clothes weren't all that was familiar about the small child in front of me. As the little girl turned around, those green eyes … locked directly onto mine; I choked on my breath as I realised, this child who was suddenly crying alone in the garden, now staring back at me, was in fact myself twenty years ago …

Chapter Two

1923 came after a post-war boom, when the economy was in a dire position for various reasons. Unemployment was increasing and men were in a good position should they hold a job with a steady income. Henry worked very long hours as a railway engineer, Flo worked from home as a dressmaker, a growing profession for women who wanted to earn their own money. Flo had several regular customers and as she worked from home, she was able to take her work wherever she moved. After several years of living with her parents, Flo and Henry had finally saved enough money to put down a small deposit on their first home. Although convenient, it was often crowded living and working in her parents' house. She had three sisters and two brothers, all her junior, and so privacy was virtually unattainable. Henry, after two long years of commuting to and from London, had his position relocated to South Woodford which gave them the initiative to move in together, leaving Flo's family home in Basildon.

South Woodford station was already established and offered stable and, reliable employment. It made sense for them to move somewhere that Henry could develop his career and build a stable future for them. Living with Flo's parents had been a quick fix for their whirl-wind romance which had hit them at the early age of seventeen. Flo was a beautiful woman with a delicate frame, short black hair and striking blue eyes. Her father's parents were both Irish so she was blessed with Irish beauty. It had been her gorgeous looks that had caught Henry's attention when he had first laid eyes on her. It was Flo's' father, John who had come across the property in South Woodford.

"This would be a grand family home", he said whilst pointing to an advert he'd found whilst reading through the For Sale section in the Daily News. John was an opinionated man who always voiced his opinions whether or not they were welcome.

He argued that with the popular train line in mere walking distance from the front door of Poultney Road, he believed that it was likely that the train routes would increase to all districts of London and further afield within the coming years. He himself had been tempted by the future prospects of moving closer to London. The properties were all beautifully constructed.

"You won't do wrong taking a look at this house," he enthused. "If I earned your salary, I would be racing you to the front door." He spoke through his wiry, black moustache, not lifting his eyes from the paper that he had resting on his lap.

"Oh John, settle down, we won't be going anywhere. You wouldn't leave this place if someone handed you the money." Dorothy always seemed to calm her husband when he fired himself up about the unnecessary.

"All I'm saying is that they should take a look. Would do the kids no harm." He replied, still fixated on the small print.

They headed out the following Wednesday afternoon, to view the property on Poultney road and it was love at first sight. Never had they imagined it would be so grand.

"This place is a real catch, perfect for commuters and for those who are starting out and want to build a family." The estate agent, Mr Brackley, was good at his job and at forty-three years old, knew how to sell pretty much any property, from rack to ruin; conscience was not in his vocabulary. All he saw were pound signs at the front door. That being said, number 106 Poultney Road was just perfect for Flo and Henry and they knew immediately that it was the house they wanted to begin the rest of their lives in.

"We'll take it!" said Henry excitedly, with very little discussion between him and his wife. He was concerned that Flo would think the price too high and out of their budget but once he knew she felt the same way about the house, he was prepared to double the deposit and would stop at nothing to make this house their new home. For the first time he would admit his father-in-law was right.

It was five weeks before they collected the keys. The process was a simple one, no chain at either end and after two years of saving they had a more than ample deposit. John and Dorothy offered some items of furniture but with so much space welcoming them, two rooms remained empty. They enjoyed decorating the bare walls and eagerly savoured the refreshing atmosphere the new decor brought to the house. They chose a subtle scheme, which seemed to be all the rage at the time. More was less and so the fact that they had few furnishings and next to no knick-knacks to clutter up their shelves, only complemented their style. They chose a gentle ivory wallpaper to cover the hallway which was complemented by a green and brown floral border. The two rooms off of this followed in similarly uncomplicated style. Flo's work room at the right side of the house, next to the kitchen was of a lighter, but flattering shade of green to the border, and the living room at the front of the house had a dirty cream coloured paper hung, both of which had the same border as the hallway. They were lucky that the kitchen was already pleasant and, with new fixtures (including a very luxurious, ultra—modern, refrigerator), it was not necessary for them to redecorate, as the plain white walls were what they would have chosen if given the choice.

They made the most of the two fireplaces which ran from the living room right through to the master bedroom; both doing a great job at heating the house through. They chose a darker scheme for the upstairs of the house and had a latte paper hung in their bedroom with a contrasting cream and black border. This scheme continued through the other rooms but instead of the coloured wallpaper, they chose plain white. It was too early in their relationship to know whether they needed to choose a more distinct colour should their family grow in the future. They had discussed having children but, as they were both working and had previously been living with Flo's parents, the time had not come for the subject to be given much thought.

Flo, took everything in her stride including the cleaning, as she'd always helped her mother with chores when she lived at home. Within no time she had settled into a routine which suited her perfectly. Whilst Henry would be at work from as early as 4am until as late as 8pm, she would alternate between making clothes and getting all of the house work done. She enjoyed cooking and Henry loved sampling new foods. Every Monday she would try a new recipe but they found that their favourite was calves' liver with a thick gravy, potatoes and veg. They became comfortable with their life together in their new home.

They spent six months of bliss living alone in number 106 before Flo shared some thrilling news with Henry.

"I'm pregnant!"

Although they'd not been trying for a baby, and had not meticulously discussed the subject, they were ecstatic to learn of their new addition. They decorated the second bedroom upstairs with cream and brown and introduced endearing farmyard animals to their novel nursery. Flo was six days later than her due date and spent twenty-five hours in labour on the seventh day of October, 1923. Henry, as always, supported her through the delivery, until the midwife asked him to wait outside, and was delighted when he re-entered the room and met their baby boy, who they called Richard.

Dorothy and John were very proud grandparents as were Vera and Les, Henry's parents, who welcomed them home with balloons and banners.

"He's adorable," John said holding tiny Richard in his arms for the first time.

"He's just perfect isn't he, just like his very clever Mummy," replied Henry, looking over at Flo who was resting on the sofa. "Now our family's complete."

The next few months were tiresome, with very little sleep shared between both parents. Richard was, although not demanding, a very hands-on child. He loved company and would cry most nights just for a cuddle and a lullaby to encourage him back to sleep. John returned to the railway immediately and so Flo took the brunt of the sleepless nights. Although most children would settle into a sleeping pattern within nine months, Richard was still waking in the early hours well past his first birthday. This put strain on Henry and Flo's relationship and meant that a second income, although important, was not always possible. Feeling exhausted most days meant that motivation to design new dresses, and fix existing ones, withered. Finally at around fifteen months old, Richard began to sleep through the nights and Flo began to get her life back to normal. Henry came home from work early one evening.

"Close your eyes," he insisted, as he pulled Flo away from her duties.

"Why?" Flo responded, slightly anxious but very excited as she knew it must be some kind of surprise; it was very rare for Henry to come home early from a shift.

"Just come downstairs and then close your eyes. I have something for you."

Flo anxiously did as she was told and stepped downstairs. Closing her eyes, Henry took her in his arms and guided her into her workroom.

He sat her down, "Now open."

Flo opened her eyes and in front of her sat the grandest sewing machine she had ever seen. It was the latest Singer machine and must have cost Henry at least one month's salary.

"Can we afford this? I know you've been doing extra shifts but... are you positive this is what you want to spend your money on?"

"I'm one hundred per cent positive and, anyway, you will make the money back in no time and you can buy me that new camera I've seen." Henry said throwing a cheeky wink in Flo's direction.

"Keep dreaming, I'd need a hundred new clients to see the money for that model. I can't believe it, thank you very much."

Flo threw her arms around Henry's shoulders, "I think you could work up to a hundred clients easily with the speed of this thing. Don't rule out a Debrie Sept just yet".

Within a month or two Flo had a regular pattern of mixing work with looking after Richard, and she was able to start rebuilding her client base and contribute by earning her own money again. They were able to decorate in line with the trends and offer Richard anything he needed. By his second birthday he was developing much faster than many of Flo's friends' children of the same age.

Flo stood at the door and waved goodbye to her son with a tear in her eye as he made his way to the bus on his first day at Bancroft school. He was very excited about making new friends and learning things in class. Richard was a very handsome child with a slim build, floppy dark hair and a outgoing personality to match. He was always dressed well and was encouraged by his peers to get involved with school activities. There was no reason for him to find it hard to make friends; but he did. He met his best friend, Harry, on his second day. Harry was a cute little boy with red hair and chubby cheeks. Lots of children would laugh at him and call him names because he looked different but Richard didn't seem to mind one bit.

"My name's Richard, what's your name?"

"Harry. My Dad's called Richard but everyone calls him Dick? Kind of like a nickname."

Richard thought about his new friend's request for a while and replied, "Yeah. Why not."

From that day on Richard and Harry were inseparable. They would meet each other on the bus each morning, tell jokes and talk about the other children in class.

"What do you think of Claire Green?" asked Harry one day on their walk home together.

"I sat next to her when we were doing art the other day and she didn't say a word to me, not even when I spoke to her about her drawing. She just looked at me and then hid her face behind her hair," Harry told Richard who was listening eagerly. "You know that people say her mum's a witch, don't you? That she speaks to dead people."

"Don't be daft. How can dead people speak? Where would she see them to talk to them? You're making it up," Richard giggled.

"I'm not telling fibs, that's the truth. I heard my mum speaking to Dad about it at the weekend, and Mum said that she doesn't want me to be in the same class as her next year as she thinks that Claire may have some kind of evil presence or something like that."

"Well I think that sounds like nonsense and you of all people should know better than to believe gossip," Richard said sharply. He hated bullies.

However irrational, Harry seemed to believe what he was saying. Richard had never heard of anything like it before and never had to deal with death. All he knew was that once you died, you were buried and would no longer be with the living. He had assumed this was all he would ever need to know.

Over the next few years Harry became one of the family and would join Richard and Flo for dinner on nights when Henry would work late. When Richard had his twelfth birthday he no longer had to take the bus to school but instead would ride his bike with Harry. They would cycle the shortest route through the fields at the back of Westfield Lane and up over the main road bridge. They took this route every day for almost three years. On July 3, 1935, Harry rang on the front door of number 106 and, just the same as every other morning, asked for Richard to join him on his ride to school. Whilst he waited downstairs, Flo offered him a duplicate of Richards's lunch; a cheese sandwich, a carton of juice and an apple.

"Thanks, Mrs Camp, this looks great."

"Not a problem Harry, only leftovers of Richard and Henry's lunches," Flo told him, as she started clearing the dishes.

"All the same, it's very kind of you putting yourself out for me, it's more than my own mother has ever done. She could learn a thing or two from you."

As a smile crept across Flo's face. Harry was an honest boy, more loyal than most his age and Flo was grateful that Richard had him as a friend. Richard came running down the stairs, grabbed his rucksack and threw his lunchbox inside.

"Thanks, Mum," he said as he kissed her on the cheek and waved her goodbye.

"You're really lucky, you know, having a mum like you've got," said Harry as they walked across the front path to their bikes.

"She's one in a million," Richard agreed. "Right; race ya!"

Both boys hopped on their bicycles, rucksacks thrown across their backs, and started on their usual route to school. They raced across the fields, both astride their saddles, hearts pounding inside their chests, thumping in their ears, faster with every minute that passed.

"I'm gonna beat you today," Harry mocked, shouting over the sound of their bicycle wheels rushing through the grass, "I'm not letting you win one more race. Enough is enough."

"I'd like to see you try! Enjoy being up ahead whilst it lasts, I'm only giving you a head start to make it a little more challenging," teased Richard, who was following closely on Harry's trail.

They were coming to the end of the field which then turned to a narrow path leading to the main road a minute or two from the school gates. Richard was just a few feet behind Harry but was a lifetime of thoughts away. He was enjoying the wind in his hair and the freedom he felt beneath the wheels of his bike. He was blissfully unaware of anyone or anything around him until suddenly something caught his attention and that someone, somewhere was watching them. He looked all around, darting his head from left to right but the field seemed as though it was empty apart from his friend who was getting further away up ahead. There it was again; out of the corner of his eye he saw something move. He turned his head to where the shift from stillness had been and could see something black emerging from behind a large oak tree about fifty feet to the left of him. The movement, although staggered, was quick and although Richard had slowed to a sluggish speed, he was still unable to see the person clearly enough to know who it was. All he did know was that the figure looked like it could be a man. No sooner had he seen him moving through the trees a few feet beside him, than the apparition disappeared. Richards's eyes searched the empty fields, desperate to see who it was, watching him and his friend; but he was gone. Through all of this, he hadn't noticed Harry stretching the distance between them and racing speedily towards the path ahead. They would usually slow down a little in case there was anyone coming in the opposite direction, as the path was narrow and not wide enough for two-way traffic.

"Harry, slow down, what are you doing? I'm serious, there's someone following us, did you see that man?" Harry either didn't hear Richards's plea or was too intent upon winning the race to the school gates to slow down.

Harry went flying through the open gate onto the gravel of the path and was out of sight.

"Damn it," cursed Richard as he felt a fire burning inside of him, a fear so immense that he found it hard to breathe as the cold air filled his lungs and froze his throat.

There he was again, about twenty feet in front of him at the opening of the path standing still and defiant, with no intention of moving out of his way. As the gap was fast closing between them, Richard could see that this person was definitely male, dressed solidly in black from his head to his feet. Although his face was exposed, his features were not prominent enough to distinguish. He was, however, sure of one thing; that this man was watching him and his friend and was intent on slowing Richard down. He stood higher from the saddle and pressed his feet as hard as he could onto the pedals to try to gain speed, desperate for the man to move out of his way.

"What do you want? Move out of my way, Mister, my bike will hit you."

As the last mound of grass left his back tyre, Richard had no choice but to close his eyes and twist the handlebars to avoid a collision. It all happened fast, his front tyre lost its grip and slid sideways, crashing his body to the ground; jolting every bone in his upper body and smashing his skull against the brittle soil. A sickness flowed through him, his body frozen, his voice lost and thought paralysed, as he heard the sound up ahead of Harry's bike smashing against the windscreen of a car.

Chapter Three

It had been thirty-six hours and Harry still hadn't woken up. His eyes had not opened since the accident and Richard was refusing to leave his bedside in case his friend might flicker an eyelid or twitch a finger. He didn't want to leave in case the doctors missed something, anything, which would mean he was going to survive. Everything kept running in circles through Richard's mind. If only they'd got the bus to school that day, if only they hadn't decided to race and Harry hadn't been determined it was his day to win the race; if only Richard hadn't been distracted by that man. Who was he? Why did he refuse to move out of his way? If he hadn't been preoccupied, then maybe he could have caught up with Harry and prevented all of this from happening.

The police had taken a statement from the man driving the saloon, who had claimed:

The boy appeared from nowhere. Before I had the chance to react and throw on my brake, he had smashed right through my windscreen. It was impossible for me to have prevented the accident.

Whether he could have prevented all of this by driving slower or reacting faster, all Richard cared about was whether his best friend was going to wake up.

He, too, had been interviewed and had told the police that he and his friend had been racing on their bikes to school, that they did this every day and had never considered the potential outcome. He'd decided not to mention the man to anyone. That was going to be something he would keep to himself until Harry woke up and he could share it with him. His friend would believe him; he may have even seen him himself.

The last day or two were distorted in Richard's mind; even the present seemed unreal. The doctors racing around him, the white walls, floors and linen all blurred into a disarray of components which made up his surroundings. It was only the bitter smell of antiseptic and strong stench of bleach that reassured him he was still alive.

The accident had happened on Monday morning and it was now late Tuesday afternoon. Henry had just arrived at the hospital to pick Richard up and take him home.

"Come on, boy, what good are you doing here?" Henry asked as he stroked the hair down on the back of his son's head. "You can't do anymore here for Harry than you can do at home. He wouldn't want you being all depressed, he would want to see you happy and smiling again, give him reason to wake up and get back to the fun things you two got up to." he encouraged, trying his best to get his son to accompany him home.

"How would he know whether I'm sad or not?" Richard retorted, unleashing his anguish on his father. "He can't hear me, he can't see me. He's not going to wake up, Dad, I just know it and if he does, I want to be the first person he sees. I want to be here for him if he needs me."

Richard's words touched Henry; he could feel his son's pain. He felt, more than ever before, that he needed to be a father to Richard. He needed to help him get through this. Much to Richard's frustration, he left the hospital to go home with the promise that he would return as soon as his friend woke up; if he ever did.

Later that night, Richard sat alone in his room. His parents had tried to distract him by playing board games and chatting about anything and everything. Flo had even cooked his favourite meal but all of it was wasted on Richard who had no interest in anything. How could he enjoy an evening knowing that his friend was in hospital because of him and his inability to ride fast enough, to have prevented the awful accident? It was around nine that evening that the phone rang and Flo took the call downstairs answering on the second ring as though she was expecting the call.

"Hello? Yes, hello Joyce. No, he's upstairs, why?" Richard heard his mother answer the phone.

So that he could hear clearly, he widened the gap between his bedroom door and the frame. It was Harry's mum, Joyce. Harry must have woken up. Flo was silent for a while allowing Joyce to speak. The call lasted no more than a few minutes and was ended with regret. Why an apology? Did Joyce blame Richard for her son's accident? Was Flo apologising on his behalf? The thought made Richard sick to the stomach as he flew down the stairs and met his mother at the bottom.

"Well? How is he? Has he asked for me? Does he remember what happened? Does he remember anything at all?" Richard poached without noticing the tears building in her eyes.

"I'm so sorry, Richard, I have some bad news." Flo began to cry.

She didn't have to say anymore. He knew that his best friend had not made it through the night and that earlier that day was the last time he would ever see him and he would never have the chance to say good bye. He was never going to be able to congratulate him for beating him to the school gates and never able to apologise for not being there when he needed him most. Although he could feel the warmth of his mother's arms drawing him tightly to her chest, nothing could console his broken heart. He felt empty and resentful towards his parents for encouraging him to leave his friend alone at the hospital. He wanted to be alone and so slowly turned and made his way back upstairs to his bedroom, leaving his mum to be comforted by Henry.

Harry's funeral came and went and the months began to pass. The seasons went through the motions, winter to spring and soon after summer came autumn, without a single day passing by that Richard wouldn't cycle to school on the same route as they always had, hoping, just once, that he would see the man who had been there on that terrible day. He looked but to no avail. Twelve months passed and it was nearing the end of his school year. Although he'd taken little interest in most of his academic subjects, he had excelled in music and had earned himself a place at The Royal Academy. He left his school friends without so much as a tear and settled into college well. Although he had no problems making friends, none of them compared to Harry. They didn't share his humour, or his fascination with photography. None of them could ever replace the friend he'd so tragically lost.

On the night Richard turned eighteen, he returned home to London to be with his parents. Flo had cooked a lavish meal and when he opened his present from them he was ecstatic.

"A Kodak 35mm Rangefinder. You shouldn't have done this. A jumper would have been enough," Richard said whilst concealing how overwhelmed he felt inside.

"Why wait until your twenty-first birthday to spoil you? Anyway your Father and I know how hard you've been working at college and we think you deserve it. It may even help with some of your projects."

"Well thanks, it means a lot. Do you mind if I go to my room now, I'd like to get this beast of a camera working." Richard said rather than asked, whilst standing up from the sofa and making his way to the door.

"He would have been proud, you know. Of how hard you've worked and how well you're doing. He would be looking down, feeling proud of the man you've become and the friend you would have always been to him," Henry said.

"Thanks, Dad." Richard answered without letting the tears that were welling up show in his eyes.

He left the room with his head hung down, heavy with thoughts of sorrow.

After the initial excitement of the extravagant gift had come and gone, Richard decided to have an early night. He wished his parents a good night's sleep and then laid in bed, under his bed covers, reading the instructions of his new gadget. It was the perfect present, there was nothing he would have wanted more. He switched off his side light, turned on to his side to face the wall and slowly drifted off to sleep.

*****

It was pitch black, as though someone had cut all of the electricity, candles and burners for miles around. There was just the dim light beaming down from the full moon that came through an opening in the clouds above. Richard could barely make out his surroundings just able to see that he was alone in a field, the same field that he had used en-route each day to school years before. Everything looked the same, or so it seemed. The outline of the trees stood above and all around him, and there ahead was the opening of the lane which led back to his house up ahead. As his eyes adjusted he realised that he was no longer alone. Maybe it was his friend, his finest friend, Harry. Perhaps he was trying to find him but was lost in the dark. Richard tried to call out to him but as his mouth opened, no words came through. Feeling unnerved, he tried to run but, seemingly paralysed, his limbs seized and he was frozen. He stood motionless and unaided in the middle of the field as the presence of someone watching him grew stronger. From nowhere, a twig or branch cracked behind him. As he managed to find the power to turn to face what was there, a million thoughts buzzed through him. Was he going to see the friend whom he'd mourned for so long? Or was his worst fate ahead of him, was he going to be reacquainted with the man who had been in this same field those years before. The man who had seemed to encourage his friend's death. He managed to swivel his feet and manoeuvre himself one hundred and eighty degrees, where he finally faced his fears. Richard managed to muster all of his strength, turned and ran. He ran as fast as his legs would carry him and the whole time he opened his ears to listen for any sound of footsteps chasing him. He was expecting to be tripped or grabbed but all that seemed to follow him was the racing wind, forcing him to run faster.

It wasn't long until he realised that the route he followed was taking him home and as he made it to the end of the field, he joined the lane which would take him to Poultney Road. When he did, he could see his house at the opposite end, standing unaccompanied by any other house. He was alone and surrounded by darkness. The pitch black had begun to circulate around him with only his house alight at the end of a very long passageway. Richard began to pick up pace and run as fast as he could but all the while he seemed to be getting further and further from home. Number 106, Poultney Road; his sanctuary.

Footsteps. Richard could suddenly hear footsteps coming up close behind him. He had no time to consider who else they may belong to besides his adversary and decided to sprint in an attempt to outrun the fate that he knew was ahead of him. A fate that his friend, Harry, had never known was coming. Subconsciously, it would seem, he had turned in the wrong direction and had started to run back to the field, back to where he had come from and he couldn't stop. As his breath became faster and harder, he realised his actions were not his own and, as he ran uncontrollably he saw up ahead the man dressed in black. Richard stopped and tried to compose himself when he could see someone, a child, cycling towards him from the opposite direction. He wasn't certain but the young boy looked like Harry, it was Harry and he was crying, screaming out to him. As he got closer, Richard could see that Harry was covered in blood, and one of his legs, which appeared to be strapped to the pedal of his bike, was mangled, broken at the thigh and hanging loose from the knee down. His tears were those of pain and yet his screams were of the purest fear. Before Richard was able to respond to his friend, his attentions turned to the man in black who was now walking towards the plummeting bike. It was now

Richard who chose to move, to turn and run towards the man and towards his friend who was soon to be in danger and then there it was, the car, the red saloon, the headlights which had taken Harry's life. Flashed up in front of Richard and smashed into his exhausted body.

*****

In an instant, Richard jumped from his pillow and grabbed the edge of his mattress for reassurance. As the sweat dripped from his forehead and his pulse slowed, he asked himself how long he had slept. It seemed like hours had passed so his parents must be asleep in bed. Whilst still gathering his thoughts, there was a distant tapping sound coming from the hallway outside his bedroom. The sound resembled a ping pong ball bouncing on a wooden floor, but with a thick carpet throughout, Richard knew this couldn't be what he heard. The continuous pattern persisted and seemed to be getting louder and closer to his room. Perplexed, Richard pulled himself to his feet and moved cautiously to the door. One of his parents must be awake, that was the only explanation, unless someone had broken into their house. Tugging slightly on the handle, the door dropped the catch and opened ajar. As soon as it did, the tapping stopped. He levered his head outside of the door frame and into the corridor which connected his parents' room at the front of the house with his room at the back, overlooking the station.

"Hello? Mum? Dad?" Richard called softly into the inert hallway.

Nothing moved nor made a sound as he was able to hear the rhythm of his father's snore coming from the opposite end of the house, confirming that his parents were still resting. There was no one awake and no one wandering the corridor. It must have been an extension of his dream. Richard stepped back from the door, closing it behind him. Before he reached the end of his bed there was an almighty thud, startling him to such an extreme that he fell to his knees and wrapped his hands around the back of his head.

He stayed there without moving for what seemed an eternity before he finally gained the courage to stand. As he turned to face the door, it slowly crept open, no more than an inch, but enough for Richard to know that there was someone on the other side pushing it open. He stood there, frozen to the thick, synthetic carpet beneath his clammy feet, unable to move as he waited for something more to happen, to see someone stood in the doorway. As he stood motionless, he felt a chill run down his spine and an ice-cold breath on his neck.

"Help me." The voice spoke and, although directly behind him, filled the entire room.

Impossible Richard thought and although petrified, he was eager to hear the voice again.

"Hello. Who's there?   Where are you?"

Rooted to the spot, Richard tried to speak to the voice again. He must have stood in the same position for almost ten minutes before eventually giving up and putting the experience down to the horrid dream he'd had before waking. He found movement in his muscles and dragged his legs over to his bed. He must have laid awake for more than an hour, replaying the evening's events in his mind. Wondering what part of his overactive imagination could have created the illusion of someone being in his house, and then in his room with him. How had the door opened by itself and what was the tremendous thud from outside his room? As he felt himself drift back to sleep, he heard the voice again; however, this time it was familiar.

"Please, Dick, I need your help."

Harry. It was Harry's voice. As he fell into the unconscious, Richard didn't have time to question whether his friend's plea was real or part of a new hallucination.

Chapter Four

Three months passed and Richard had started working as an apprentice for a local photographer, Leonard Prince. He had finished his college course early and had been taken under Prince's wing. He spent most of his time taking photographs but, as a hobby and for a bit of extra cash, shooting weddings and portraits. His ambition was to start his own trade, enabling him to afford the down payment to buy a place of his own.

Leonard asked if Richard would cover him at his brother's wedding as he, himself, would be attending. It would be a cash job and therefore an addition to his savings. It was only a small affair but it was experience none-the-less. Still living at home, Richard had to accept work wherever he could find it and besides the photography job, he only had the evening when he played the piano at the Old Bell, a charming pub that combined typical London punters with the warmth of an open fire and the appeal of rustic beams.

Music was a passion of his and something he'd become fond of from a young age. His parents kept a baby grand piano in the downstairs lounge which had been handed down to them from the generation before. Over the years, Richard had become more acquainted with the instrument and was able to play music by ear from the age of ten. He would often play to his parents' friends when they came to visit. Word soon got round of his talent and it wasn't long after he returned home from College that the proprietor of the Old

Bell, John Bishop, got in touch with Richard to arrange a regular slot for him to play to his punters.

Arriving at the Holy Trinity Church in Woodford at eleven-thirty that morning, he was able to set up and test shots he would later take of the bride and groom. One thing he loved about working for Leonard was his collection of cameras; today he would get to use the mighty Kodak Ektra. He could spend hours playing around with gadgets, and cameras were his favourite kind. It was such a beautiful day that Richard was able to take his borrowed camera outside and have a wander through the graveyard. It was a quaint church that was embellished with glorious sculptures and statues overlooking the graves. Richard enjoyed capturing the everlasting expressions of the effigies that stood so grandly in such a sensitive abode. The statue of a woman, or mother that clung tightly to her child, had been erected above a headstone that read, Loved so much, taken too soon. I will love you forever. There is great beauty within a graveyard, and Richard believed that it had many similarities to a photo album; a place which could stand still in time, initially visited by people, loved ones, enabling them to remember moments, places or people. A dwelling that will continue and never change over time. A place to forget the present and see through the eyes of the past. As Richard moved from each monument; the proud man, the crying child, snapping away at the beautiful surroundings, he was drawn back to reality on hearing the recognisable laughter of his boss,

Leonard. He grabbed his equipment and made his way through the graveyard to the church entrance.

As people continued to arrive, they were greeted with a smile and a click of the camera capturing their gleaming expressions of anticipation. There had been little briefing of the sort of portfolio the couple expected and, with such high recommendation from Leonard, Richard was able to explore his abilities and shoot freely. Focusing on guests, particularly those who enjoyed the attention, he had almost forgot to prepare for the bride's arrival.

The day ran smoothly, from wedding vows to reception drinks, a glorious wedding breakfast and, as Richard said his goodbyes, he was thanked profusely by the bride's father who offered him a rather generous gratuity for his efforts. Leaving with more than a month's wages in his back pocket, Richard stopped at the local newsagents to grab a packet of cigarettes on his way home. Smoking was a habit he'd picked up at college and hadn't been able to shake.

"Just these then, Dick? You cutting back?" asked Jack Morris, the owner of the Woodford News and a good friend.

"Yes, just those, thanks, and no, no cut backs. You know how it is, my Mum hates smoking, so I'm busy tonight with work; the cigarettes would only be a distraction", replied Richard. "Probably be a good thing for my health, I'm sure. See you tomorrow no doubt."

"Yes, tomorrow, take care.

Richard was home by eight and was greeted by an empty house and a note,

Gone out for dinner, be home before midnight. Vegetable stew in the pan. Mum x

Both Richard and Henry had so far escaped being drafted but they never took that for granted, they were always expecting a call-up. Rationing had affected everyone living in London but Flo had always been careful with money and so too she was with rationing, using only the bare minimum.

As Richard began heating the stew, he poured himself a small glass of brandy, a tipple he'd taken to over the past couple of months. He set himself a table place and finished off the stew, which happened to be delicious even if it was missing a vital ingredient, it was just what he needed after a long day. Throwing his plates to the washing up bowl, he made his way upstairs and into the attic room at the top of the house. It was mostly empty, besides a musky smell that lingered in its air. As it was pretty dark up there, it was the perfect atmosphere to develop film. As he'd received such generosity, he wanted to ensure that he got an early start on developing the film with enough time to guarantee he got the best from the photographs he'd taken. He spent much time on the development process to ensure that he didn't lose a single frame.

It was during this process that he saw him.

"Impossible," he whispered aloud as he studied the photograph that he himself had just developed.

From within the image stood a slender figure with a head of strawberry blonde hair. It was impossible, but undeniably him; he was wearing the same clothes he had on that day; that tragic, awful day. From behind one of the many crumbling gravestones, standing facing the camera lens, was unquestionably Richard's childhood friend, his best friend. Harry.

Unable to believe his eyes, Richard quickly lifted more of the photographs, one after the other, searching for more of his dead friend, but no more appeared. He desperately wanted to find more photos which would confirm what was in front of him and what his eyes were telling him. That somehow, beyond the bounds of possibility, his deceased friend was able to show himself through a photograph. But, out of more than twenty shots he'd taken alone in the graveyard, Harry had chosen to appear in just one. Did this mean that Harry was following him that morning, watching his every move?

Richard sat alone in the attic room for some time, re-evaluating the negative, wanting to ensure that it was real and that he hadn't blended two negatives together but this, he was sure, was not possible. It had to be real. Alone in the darkness, he asked himself questions, ones which made him feel uneasy. Why was Harry still here and unable to rest? Was it that he had unfinished business or was he trapped here? Could it be that he blamed Richard for what happened that day, for the accident? Or perhaps because he left his bedside when he died and when he needed him the most. Richard felt a chill running through him.

"I'm sorry, Harry, I'm so sorry." As he spoke these words aloud he heard a faint tapping sound coming from the room below.

He raised his head and focused on the beating rhythm but, the instant he did, the noise changed and became a closer, dragging sound which vibrated on the floor beneath his feet. Richard stood, slowly, and walked cautiously across the pitch black room, following the safe boards laid on the floor to the loft hatch which was open and led to the first floor landing. Perhaps his parents were home but although he wasn't sure what the time was, he didn't think it was much past nine and he hadn't heard them come in.

"Hello?" he asked into the blackness of the empty hallway. "Mum? Dad? Is that you?"

He climbed down the ladders and made his way across the floor to the light switch. He'd always wondered why the switch was on the opposite side of the hall to where the bedrooms were, it made it difficult at night if he woke up and needed to feel his way to the bathroom. All the time he was making his way down the hall, he was following the awful, scraping sound which now appeared to be coming from the back bedroom, behind a closed door which led to a room which was, to his knowledge, empty. When from nowhere the sound stopped, resulting in a pure, echoing silence. You might imagine that this would ease the tension within Richard's stomach but the stillness only made his foreboding worse. It was only then that he was hit with an abrupt stench, a smell so vile that he lost his breath for a few seconds. Unable to recognise the odour, he was immediately aware that every hair on both his arms and neck was standing perfectly on end and a freezing current of air passed through him. Before he was able to think, to try to justify the phenomenon, he felt a hand on his neck, around his throat, strangling him, forcing him to his knees. He desperately fought against the strength of something, or someone, that he wasn't able to see. As he frantically tried to win the endless battle, his face crashed against the cold, rough carpet and he took what he thought would be his last breath.

*****

A brilliant light blinded his eyes. It was a white light that burned through his pupils, blazing his retinas. He closed his eyes tight and slowly opened them to see if they would adjust to the intensity of the light which surrounded him. As he pulled his eyes open, he was in darkness, a stark obscurity which frightened him tremendously. As his eyes focused he began to recognise his surroundings. He saw that he was in a large, open field. Somewhere that he'd visited a hundred times before, every day for so many years and that he reminisced on the time he shared there with his best friend, Harry. As he looked around he realised that the field had

51

changed dramatically from when he was last there. It had aged. The trees were withered and had shed all of their leaves; the grass, which had once been a lush green, was yellowing and much had turned to mud. It was dark, pitch black, and he was alone. His eyes scurried for the path which led in and out of the arena but it was nowhere to be seen. The panic set in fast as he tried to run, to get away from this horrifying yet familiar territory, but his feet were weighed down and he was unable to move. He wrenched at his legs but to no avail as he became heavier and less mobile as the minutes passed. In the distance he became aware that something or someone was rapidly making their way towards him. In a haze, he was able to identify the movement to be that of a person, a child in fact, running; seemingly hysterical, throwing his legs one in front of the other. As Richard focused, he made out a second figure, a much larger form, a man dressed in black. Richard froze, unable to breathe, terrified by what he saw in front of him. As the two images grew closer, Richard recognised the child to be Harry but he looked so different from the carefree, innocent boy he'd known all those years ago. The child in front of him had aged too but without getting any older. His face had become grey with a sickening fear which now overwhelmed his expression, until he saw Richard. When the child's empty eyes locked onto Richard's, his face scrunched into hatred, into a sorrow which appeared to be drowned by disgust. He was running directly towards him, faster, eager to get to him. Struggling to move, Richard was breathing hard, now terrified by the two apparitions moving closer towards him. Even more terrifying than the man in black was the old child who was running at him and had the darkest, most hateful look in his eyes.

*****

When Richard woke up, it was already past five in the afternoon. The light was pushing its way through the open curtains. He was lying on top of his bed, fully dressed in the brown trousers and cream and brown striped shirt he had worn the previous day. How had he got there? Instantly, memories from the night before came flooding back to him. The intermittent dragging sound that came from the back bedroom and then that chill, that force he couldn't see, and was unable to fight. He remembered being forced to his knees and struggling for breath as he must have lost consciousness, but how had he ended up in bed? Had his parents come home and thought he was drunk? He got up and straightened himself out and made his way to the bathroom.

"Good morning sleepy head. You were out for the count when we got home last night, I thought you might've stayed on late at the wedding? Did you not feel well?" his mother asked as she made her way up the stairs towards him, carrying a pile of clean laundry.

Richard just stared at her. He'd felt fine last night, he hadn't drunk, besides a small tipple and it took more than that to have an effect on him. He remembered eating the

53

meal his mother had prepared and then being intent on developing his films. That was it, he remembered. The photographs of the graveyard, the child he had recognised. His childhood friend, Harry whose life had come to such a tragic end had been in his photograph.

"Impossible …" Richard muttered.

"Pardon? What's wrong, Richard, you don't look well." Flo responded with concern.

"Mum, I'm fine, I have to get ready. I'm playing over the road this afternoon, I was meant to be there ages ago."

Richard kissed his mother on the cheek and made his way to the bathroom. He had to wash away his thoughts from the night before. The last thing he wanted right now was to be reminded of that ghostly photograph.

It was just before seven when he arrived at the Old Bell and John had just about given up on him.

"Here he is, the man we've all been waiting for. Richard, you're late and the punters are waiting. We have an eager crowd this evening." John stressed. "You're going to have to stay late," he muttered under his breath.

The Old Bell was a small pub and most of its customers were regulars and men well into their fifties. Unlike many other pubs in London, it had a very welcoming atmosphere for anyone who drank there.

"That's fine, I'm sorry I'm late, I had a heavy night." He replied quietly so that the clientele wouldn't hear them. "Hello, ladies and gents, my apologies, I hope you're all enjoying your drinks. I'm going to start by playing you my favourite song, 'Somewhere Over the Rainbow' but should you have any recommendations, please just make a request."

As he began to play, the music swept through him, his body moving to the rhythm as he was swallowed by the melody. People listened silently as they always did for a moment or two, but soon a low hubbub settled in the room. Richard had always played by memory and allowed it to take him through every tune, always perfect, never missing a note.

As he played he could feel someone staring at him. Curious to see who was burning a hole in his back, he casually peeped over his left shoulder. To his delight, his gaze was met by that of a pair of piercing blue eyes. Sitting with two other girls was a beautiful woman with long blonde hair and eyes so deep he could have lost himself in them. He very nearly lost concentration but managed to keep up with the music he played. He hadn't ever seen this girl before and yet she was the most fine-looking woman to have caught his eye. As their eyes caught each other's, he felt obliged to look away, not wanting to intrude upon her privacy but before he did, she offered him a smile which he returned before resuming to the music he played.

Richard played for forty minutes, mainly requests, before taking a break. As he left his piano stool, he was greeted by a porcelain face and hourglass figure. It instantly occurred to him that this was the beauty who had caught his eye earlier.

"Hello," said Richard, although his voice sounded mousy and anything but confident.

"Hi, my name's Ellen but everyone calls me Eileen. I just wanted to say how wonderful I think you play and that 'Over the Rainbow' is my favourite song, and you did it justice. It sounded magnificent. So, thank you."

And before he could reply she had turned on her heel and headed back to her friends, grabbed her coat and left. It was right then that he had met the woman he would spend the rest of his life with, the woman who would share all of his secrets, his talents and his troubles. This woman was Ellen Chenery and he made it his mission that it would not be long before he saw her again. That night he returned home with not so much as a thought of his poor friend, the one who was trapped in the photograph that he had tucked away in his room. He thought only of the enigmatic woman he had met that evening, and fell asleep lulled by peaceful thoughts of her.

Chapter Five

The sun rose early the next morning and, as Richard stirred, his first thoughts were of the beautiful woman he had met the previous evening. He desperately wanted to find out who she was, and in particular, if she was seeing anyone. So instead of spending the day developing the wedding photographs or perhaps investigating the inexplicable appearance of his dead best friend in the graveyard, he chose to focus his attentions on Ellen. He remembered seeing her speaking to John at the Old Bell the previous evening whilst he was playing so decided to quiz him about his prospective love interest.

He knocked on the bar door, the entrance John's friends or locals used. Within minutes he was greeted by a weary-eyed barman.

"Morning John, I've got a favour to ask," Richard said and, receiving no reply, continued, "that woman, the blonde-haired lady who was in here last night with her friends, I saw her speaking to you. Do you know her well?"

"Bloody hell, Richard, calm down. You sound like a bloody prowler. Why do you want to know? If I'm honest I thought I was in there, I think she may have a thing for older men, you know…"

"Oh don't be so ridiculous. Come on, John, help me out here. You must know who she is, it can't be the first time she's been in here. I really like her."

It was the first time in years that Richard had let his feelings show to anyone about anything. He needed John's help and he'd do anything to get it.

"OK, calm down," John replied with a smirk. "Her name is Ellen Chenery if you didn't already know and she lives the other side of the station, Harpers Road. Not sure of the number but she did say she would be back up here tonight. I think she liked the entertainment," he said, winking at a rather bemused Richard. "I'm referring to you playing the piano, you daft plonker! Do you fancy playing tonight?"

"No, not tonight, I have more important things to attend to." Richard replied. He shook John's hand and left, wishing the day away.

*****

Soon enough evening had arrived and an acceptable time to head to the pub without looking like he had a problem with alcohol. He'd spent the afternoon working on the Princes' wedding photographs and was pretty impressed by his handiwork. He still hadn't given any more thought to the other photos. Instead, he chose to develop the rest of the photographs of people enjoying their lives and each other. He didn't want to think about the possibility that there may be more to life and, in fact, more to death. He didn't want to think about that.

He threw on his best trousers, white shirt and cardigan and headed over to the Old Bell with every hope he would see her. The woman who had caught his eye, invaded his every thought and encouraged the first peaceful, unbroken sleep in longer than he could remember. He pushed open the heavy wooden door and there she was, sitting in the same dingy corner she had been the night before, looking even more radiant than he remembered. He thought it best to play it cool and order himself a drink before going over to make his move.

Something Richard had never been was a ladies' man. He wasn't used to making the first move, or making any move come to think of it. He was hopeless when it came to women and, with very little experience, he didn't want to seem desperate.

"I'll have an IPA please, John. A pint, I think I need it."

"Don't be silly," John could feel his friend's nerves, "just play it cool, go and have a chat with her. I can tell she wants you to go over, she's not taken her eyes off you since you walked in."

"Don't be daft John, but thanks for the encouragement," Richard retorted and, as he turned to face her, he saw that John was telling the truth, she was looking over and their eyes locked once again.

"Hi," Richard took Ellen's hand and kissed it slowly. She giggled. "I didn't think I'd see you in here again," he said as he sat down beside her.

"I moved close by a few months ago with my parents, so I suppose this is my local. How come you aren't playing again this evening? You really are very good."

Richard felt himself blush. "Thanks, but tonight's my night off. I work full time as a photographer and on a Saturday I like to play piano for the locals in here. What do you do?"

As Ellen opened up to Richard about her ambitions to be a nurse and her dreams of having a family and settling down, the hours soon passed and it was almost ten o clock. Her friends had already left and there were only two other men who were sitting down the other end of the bar.

"Why is it you're here alone, Richard? Don't your friends come out on a school night?" she teased.

Richard grew thoughtful for a moment or two, his mind traipsing through memories of so many men who had tried to befriend him over the years, tried to get close but he would always have his guard up, not lowering it for anyone.

"I lost my best friend years ago. I blame myself and I suppose I'm scared to let anyone in, frightened that if anyone gets too close to me again, I would lose them too and I don't think I could bear to go through that again. I have friends, people I can turn to but I prefer to do some things alone. Like come to the pub, and look how lucky that's turned out to be." Richard gazed into Ellen's eyes.

This woman was like no one he'd ever met, he had only known her a few hours yet he already felt close to her; like he could tell her anything.

"Be here tomorrow, the same time?" she asked.

"Most certainly," Richard replied, trying to hide the delight in his voice.

*****

The following night and the subsequent two nights, they met for a drink and sat for hours talking about their pasts, the complications of childhood, and the delights of the future. Ellen came alone on Friday night which was a good sign.

"So, Richard, tell me, you live just round the corner but you are yet to invite me to meet your parents. Are you not proud to be in my company?" Ellen asked with a straight face.

"Most certainly I am but I'm unsure whether or not you would refuse my request, and I wouldn't want to impose anything upon you." Richard replied, not really knowing how to respond to her question. "You could come back now and I'll introduce you. They won't mind, it's not too late," he glanced at his watched, "8 o'clock. Come on, I'm excited now. They'd love to meet you."

With that, he grabbed her hand and led her out of the pub, across the road and to his house down Poultney Road. He explained how he'd lived in the house his whole life and that his parents bought it when they first got married. As they reached the front door, Ellen looked up at the tall town house.

"Wow, it's a big house for just three of you," she stated.

"I suppose so, come on in."

As they stepped into the house, the lights were out and it was dark.

"They must be out. Sorry, Ellen, we can leave if you want?" Richard asked.

"No, no. Do you have any tipple here? I would love a gin and tonic," she said as she walked into the front room, sat down and made herself at home.

"Yeah, sure, stay here, I'll just go pour you a drink."

He ran through to the kitchen and grabbed the half-empty bottle of gin from the liquor cupboard, poured two glasses and topped with tonic and ice and ran to join Ellen in the lounge.

"Perfect," she said as she sipped on her double strength drink. "Are you trying to get me drunk, Mr... What's your full name? I think that's possibly the only thing I've not asked you."

"Camp. Richard Camp." He replied and as he did Ellen leant across the sofa and kissed him.

She never knew it but that was the first kiss he had ever shared with a woman. He placed his hand on her knee and reciprocated the caress. He lost himself in the moment, embraced her face with his hands and enjoyed her stroking the back of his neck, tickling the tip of his spine with her fingertips. Her touch felt so warm and soft against his skin, he could have let her stroke him for hours on end. His hands left her face and travelled along the length of her shoulder, down her arms and then intertwined his fingers with hers. He had never felt like this before, so utterly infatuated.

"What was that?" Ellen jumped as she pulled away from their embrace.

"What was what?" Richard began to answer but was interrupted by what sounded like crying; a child crying, and it was coming from inside the house on the first floor landing.

He let go of Ellen's hand and stood slowly from the sofa.

"It's coming from upstairs, Richard, are your parents' home?" Ellen asked frantically.

Richard didn't reply but raised his hand to silence her. He knew that his parents weren't home, he didn't need to reassure himself of that, he was already certain that someone was in the house with them. He made his way out of the lounge and into the hallway looking up the tall, twisted flight of stairs. The lights were off so it was very hard to see but, by following the sound of sobbing, he was able to find his way through the dark. He was aware that Ellen was mimicking his every move and he was too comforted by her company to ask her to leave. Although he was apprehensive as to what was in his house, he felt reassured that he wasn't alone. Slowly he began to make his way up the stairs, he had never before noticed how steep the stairs were; so much so that he had to make a conscious effort to climb each step, one at a time, each one seeming higher and more difficult to climb.

"Hello?" He asked into the darkness, "Is anyone there?"

There was silence; the crying stopped and no one answered, all that could be heard was the sound of Ellen faintly breathing by his side.

"Perhaps we should leave Richard, something doesn't feel right."

As she spoke, there was the faintest sound of footsteps running swiftly across the hall. Tiny footsteps, like a child's. The moonlight crept in through the back bedroom and, as it did, it highlighted a piece of white paper in the middle of the hall.

"What's that?" asked Ellen, who had managed to catch her breath.

"I don't know," Richard replied as he moved his upper body forward to grab the piece of paper.

As he did he was able to see that it wasn't paper; it was in fact a photograph, one that he had developed.

As he lifted the picture, he saw what he had hoped he wouldn't see, the face of his unforgettable friend,

"Harry," he whispered, and with that the photograph caught fire in his hand and began to burn away in front of them.

*****

He had no idea how or why it had happened, but the photographic evidence he had of his dear friend, physically caught alight in the palm of his hand and disintegrated to ash in front of both of them. They spoke in length about possible explanations, both rational and irrational. They even considered spontaneous combustion, but dismissed the idea as it seemed a little too far-fetched. Richard told Ellen everything. About the death of his best friend, that he wasn't there when he died and even about the man in black.

"It's obvious; your own conscience is haunting you. Making you feel guilty for what happened all those years ago. You must have left the photo there earlier, or perhaps your parents found it before they left and it slipped out of their hands."

"But what about the crying? You heard it too, don't try to deny it. It's not the first time either. I've felt like someone… something has been watching me for a while. Not just in my dreams but when I'm here alone, or out by myself. And how do you explain the picture? Ellen, there is no explanation, I've questioned every plausible option and there aren't any left. I've never believed in ghosts or the afterlife, I've never had to discuss anything like it with anyone before tonight but it's the only reasonable explanation I have."

"You really do think it's Harry's ghost coming back to you? I suppose that could explain the noises and the photographs, but I'm not sure of the whole idea. It seems a little unbelievable to me. There has to be some …"

"Logical explanation? I promise you there isn't and, although he was my friend, it's the only time in my life I feel scared, the night when he woke me in my sleep, just now, upstairs. It's like he wants me to do something but I don't know what." Richard sat for a moment, thinking, asking himself the same questions over and over again.

"You could ask him." Ellen suggested. "I know that a couple of my friends once tried something called a Ouija board, only for a laugh and nothing happened, but apparently if there is a ghost there and you call it, then they can come through the Ouija board and communicate with you. I would do one with you, it might be fun."

"I'm not sure, Ellen, would you know how to make one or what one looks like?" Richard asked.

"Yeah, numbers and letters around the outside and a yes, no and exit in the middle. If you have any spare pieces of cardboard, or even better would be wood, then I can make one now if we have time?"

Richard considered what they were about to do and asked himself whether or not it was a good idea. Although he was doubtful it would work, there was still something inside him screaming out not to start something that he may not be able to finish. He thought momentarily about what might happen if it were to work and his friend was able to contact him. What would he say? Would he blame his death on Richard for not being there when he needed him the most, for not staying with him in hospital when he died? Was it a good idea to delve into something he knew nothing about? On the other hand, he had the opportunity of contacting someone he once loved so dearly, he could find out why he was haunting him and perhaps be able to help him rest. He seemed to have convinced himself of the idea and ran to find some wood; he knew there would be some in the shed. He found some and gave it to Ellen, with a pen, and allowed her to create the Ouija board. It didn't take her long and before he knew it she had laid it on the family coffee table.

"You got a glass?" she asked. "One that's free from liquor." Gesturing at her own glass, "It's lucky we never got round to drinking these," she explained, "you're supposed to be of a sober mind, not influenced by alcohol," she said, sharing a smile. "OK, so we both place our fingertips on the glass and close our eyes. You can ask questions, and the ghost should respond by moving the glass to spell things out or answer yes or no to questions. You ready?"

"Let's get this over with," he pleaded.

They both placed their fingertips lightly onto the top of the glass and sat in the still silence for a minute or two.

"What happens now?" Richard asked.

"You wait, I did say it mightn't work, I'm not sure how reliable these things are. Just be patient."

Patient they were as they sat for at least twenty minutes, before both started to grow increasingly agitated.

"I don't think anything's going to happen, Richard, maybe you need to ask something."

"Like what?"

"If there's anyone there, give us a sign. If there's anyone there, give us a sign." Ellen began to repeat over and over until Richard joined in and their words became a chant.

Within minutes, they both felt a heat from within the glass, burning so hot it was unbearable to touch. They looked at each other and broke the chant into a silence as the glass began to move. It started off slowly.

"You're doing that aren't you, Ellen? Stop messing with the glass."

"It's not me, I'm barely touching it, I promise."

They both watched in sheer amazement, unable to believe their eyes as Richard felt a glimpse of anticipation. Would this be his chance to rectify his friend's unhappy ending? Would he be able to help his friend rest in peace after all these years? The glass picked up speed and they could only watch whilst it moved across the board where it sat at the letter M. It stayed still for a second or two and then darted quickly across the board to the letter A, then N; then I, N, B, L. This can't be happening, Richard thought as he watched the glass speed over to A, it can't be. It must be some kind of joke. He had told Ellen what had happened that day and what he had seen, perhaps it was her idea of a joke. C, he could hardly breathe as it spelt out the last, dreaded letter of the word, K.

"Man ... in .... Black." Ellen spelt aloud, "Man in Black, Richard, did you see that? Did you see?"

But before she could continue, the glass started to move again, this time with more speed; it almost glided between letters as it spelt out W.A.T.C.H.I.N.G.

Before it moved anymore, Richard let go of the glass, stood from the floor and threw the board across the room.

"Ellen, it's time I took you home."

69

As she lived just around the corner, Richard walked her home. He was a gentleman and kissed her hand on the doorstep, not hanging around to meet her parents. It was almost ten and he didn't want them thinking that he would make a habit of keeping her out late; besides, he needed to be by himself, he wasn't any company to be around. He had to go through the events that had happened that evening. If what had happened that night had been real and Ellen wasn't winding him up and it wasn't some part of their imagination running away with them both, then it was possible his worst fears had been realised. Instead of contacting Harry, he had connected with his nemesis, the man, or thing that he feared the most, more than anything else in the whole world. The man in black; was it him who had been in his house earlier that evening, was he the one who had woken him the other night? Or was Harry trying to tell him something about the man in black? He wasn't going to know for sure. He did, however, know how delighted he was to see that his parents were home and the lights were on upstairs; but all the time his subconscious reminded him that it wasn't just his parents who were inside waiting for him.

Chapter Six

It became a regular thing, that Ellen and Richard would spend an evening together and although they rarely spoke of what happened the night they used the Ouija board, just as they didn't share their secret with anyone; there wasn't a day that passed that they didn't think about what happened. They had been dating for about six months when Richard proposed to Ellen. He had known from the moment he met her that he would spend the rest of his life with her and he didn't intend to waste more time waiting to do the inevitable. Ellen was delighted and answered yes without hesitation. They planned a simple wedding and only invited family and their closest friends to share their day with them. As they had very little money between them, it was decided that they would share the house on Poultney Road with Richard's parents, claiming Richard's adolescent bedroom as their marital residence. It wasn't long before Ellen found out she was pregnant and they had their first son, Robert. The space was tight in number 106 and so they converted the lower floor sitting room into a nursery.

They had been living in the house for about fourteen months and the situation was working out fine. Flo and Henry would use the living space most of the time whist Richard and Ellen spent time with Robert in his large nursery. Richard now worked for himself as a freelance photographer and barely had time to play the piano anymore at the Old Bell. It was almost two years since his attempt to contact the dead and he hadn't experienced anything since. He had convinced himself that everything had been the result of his own imagination. That ever since his friend died, he had blamed himself and created an illusion around him which enabled him to blame himself further by thinking that the spirit of his dead friend Harry blamed him as well. Once he and Ellen settled down and Robert came along, his mind was occupied with other things and he no longer had time to make believe in ghosts.

"I should be home around six this evening, Mum and Dad will be home later, about nine I think. I said that I would only stay until the speeches are finished, so I may be home earlier," Richard said whilst planting a kiss on his wife's head. "Be a good boy for Mummy, Robert, Daddy will see you tonight."

"OK, good luck today and we'll see you later. Wave goodbye to Daddy," Ellen said, waving her son's hand, back and forth, whilst Richard walked out the front door. "Just me and you today, baby. What shall we do?"

She made Robert's formula milk which much to everyone's dismay, seemed to work better for her than breast milk. Once fed, Robert lay blissfully on his play mat and enjoyed kicking his feet in the air with his mum cleaning up around him. Ellen's life had changed dramatically over the past eighteen months and that was all down to Richard. She was grateful to him for giving her a life that she had always dreamed of. Although they couldn't yet afford their own home, they shared a big house with Flo and Henry whom she adored and who loved her and Robert. He was a blessing and one that she considered herself lucky to have. As she continued to think about her blissful life, she unconsciously ploughed her way through the housework. It was part of the set-up. They paid nominal rent but had to take care of the house, keep it clean and do their fair share of cooking. Ellen didn't mind but she didn't have any experience in the kitchen. Her Mum was a great cook but she never had the time or the patience to sit down and show Ellen the way about a kitchen so most of her recipes were works in progress. Tonight she was making sausage casserole; it was one meal that she found fairly easy to make and always resulted in clean plates and, because Henry and Flo were eating out, she could take her time and not have to hurry to get the dinner on the table.

Time always seemed to pass quickly when she was home alone, busy with housework and before she knew it was almost four, Richard would be home in a couple of hours so she needed to get dinner on. She carried Robert to his cot in the nursery at the front of the house and laid him down where he continued to sleep peacefully. She stood for a moment, looking down at him and his little rounded face that perfectly held all of his tiny features faultlessly. She smiled to herself, proud, as she walked out of the room and closed the door ajar behind her. Although the house was big, the rooms were large and so carried every little noise through the house so, when Robert cried, she was confident that she would be able to hear him from anywhere in the house. She returned to the kitchen and began preparing dinner. It was whilst she was chopping the onions that the crying started. She didn't rush to his aid as she believed in leaving him to cry it out. As it was almost five, she didn't have the time to comfort Robert and needed to finish dinner, she would let his tears tire him. It didn't last long, which surprised her. Within just minutes, his tears had turned to gurgles. This bothered her more than when he was crying. She put down her knife and slowly walked out of the kitchen and into the narrow hallway which lead to the nursery. As she got closer, she saw that the door was closed completely; she could have sworn that when she left Robert earlier, she left the door ajar. As she got closer, she could hear Robert's cute baby giggle which he only usually did when his Dad would pull a funny face or do a silly dance but Richard wasn't home and, as far as she was aware, Robert was in his nursery alone. Part of her wanted to rush into the room and ensure that her child was safe but something inside her pulled her back; made her consider her every move. She took each, single step slowly, gradually getting closer as she reached for the handle and put her ear against the cold wooden door. Silence. She couldn't hear a thing which was worse than hearing something, anything so she gradually pushed down the handle. As the door released, her eyes immediately travelled to where her baby should have been sleeping but instead of the pine wooden frame of her child's cot, she saw a woman, at least she thought it was female. She wore a long cream gown that covered her feet, which she noticed were not touching the ground. Her upper body was slim and her shoulders protruded through the

74

sleeves of the dress as she leaned over the cot. Standing behind this skeletal apparition, Ellen was momentarily stunned by the image. She walked towards the cot where her child was, although at that moment she couldn't see him as this woman was blocking her view. As she moved around the spectre, Ellen was horrified as she saw that the woman's thick, long grey hair was falling down and around her young child as he laid there, transfixed upon the figure. Ellen gasped as the woman raised her head, and Ellen was greeted by a face that was empty of features. There were holes where her eyes should have been and a raised bone in place of her nose. Her mouth was covered over entirely by smooth white skin and, as Ellen analysed what there was to see of her face, this figure of a woman slowly moved away from the cot, away from Ellen and towards the back wall of the room where she spread against it and disappeared.

Ellen grabbed Robert from his cot as he burst into tears and she carried him out of the house. She didn't care where she waited, but she had no intention of going back in alone. It was getting dark and was likely to be time Richard would be returning home from work. Luckily the air was warm and she was able to sit outside on the front porch. She felt safer there than she ever would now inside the house. She played the situation over in her mind again and again and every time she came to the same conclusion, that what she had just seen inside her family home was a female spirit watching over her child. She couldn't consider it an attack, nor did she feel threatened, but she did feel terrified when she thought about what the spirit could want from her child. Every time she thought about her face, that empty hollow face that was nothing but a blank canvas, she felt sick to her stomach. She couldn't wait for Richard to come home; it must be six o'clock by now. As she sat thinking, Robert began to cry, he would probably be hungry but his formula was in the fridge, inside the house. She tried her very best to comfort him and sang to him his favourite nursery rhymes but the tears continued to fall and the screams got louder, she even noticed the neighbour opposite looking from behind her curtains. She had no choice but to take him back inside. She walked along the porch to the door and turned her key in the lock. The huge front door opened and, as she peered around it, everything inside appeared normal. There was nothing out of place, no creepy images, nothing; just her slightly dark and dingy family home. She crept around the door and closed it behind her.

It wasn't long before Richard was home; he came in through the front door, pretty pink carnations in hand as if nothing had happened.

"Sorry I'm late, darling, the buses were behind time and I promised to have a quick pint with Jim after work and we got talking. You know how it is and anyway, I'm sorry. How was your day?" he asked as he lent forward and kissed her on her cheek.

Ellen looked up at him without saying a word, not because she was angry with him for making her wait, terrified and alone out on the porch, nor for not being home on time and making her have to re-enter a house that she was so afraid of, but because she couldn't find the words to describe what had happened that day. How could she begin to explain her paralysis and lack of instinct to run in and save their child when she knew he may have been in danger? Or how this woman, or ghost, or whatever she was, vanished into thin air. Would he believe her? Did she even want him to know after all of the stress and trouble he had with accepting his friend's death?

"Ellen what's wrong? Is Robert OK? How comes his crib's in the kitchen with you? What's happened?"

As he asked more questions, Ellen began to cry. They weren't tears of confusion but of relief that her husband was home with her, and she felt safe for the while.

She decided to start at the beginning and explained how she was in the kitchen when she had the feeling that she and Robert weren't alone in the house, and that someone was with him in the nursery. She explained of how she had been frozen and unable to run or react in a way that she would previously have assumed she would; and she described what had happened in that room and how the woman, or ghost, had looked. Once she'd finished, she sat back in her chair and stared at Richard, waiting for his response. Would he laugh or cry, be annoyed with her for not protecting their son in a way that he would have done? Instead he just sat for a moment looking at Robert, asleep in his cot.

"Are you sure, Ellen? Are you sure it wasn't just shadows or reflections from the road outside? People are walking past all day and their reflections could easily come through the windows."

"You don't believe me?" Ellen retorted.

"Of course I believe you but I'm trying to look at this from every angle before I go completely mad."

They sat in silence for a while, trying to regain some composure, and only then was it that Richard began to associate the Ouija board they had used years before with what had happened that day to his wife and child.

"We contacted someone else," Richard said, "We must have contacted someone other than Harry."

"What do you mean, Richard, when?" Ellen asked.

"When we were dating, you showed me how to do a Ouija board and we thought that we might contact Harry and although we weren't successful in what we'd set out to do, the Ouija board did what it was supposed to; it contacted the dead. We drew something in, Ellen, that's who, or what you saw today. She ... it, was a ghost. Something we contacted that day," he blurted. "I don't know why it's waited until now to show itself but if you are completely sure what you experienced was real, then that could be an explanation?"

Ellen sat speechless for a minute or two, unable to comprehend her husband's analogy but deep down she had a feeling that what he was saying was true.

"I think you're right. What I saw today couldn't have been human although I'm entirely sure it was real. It was Robert that made me come in, I knew something or someone was in the house before I opened the door. I could sense it, I don't know how but something inside me knew that we weren't alone."

"Did you feel threatened? Are we safe living here?" Richard asked.

"Although I was frightened, I couldn't say that I felt threatened or even that I was fearful for the safety of our son. It just felt peculiar," Ellen replied. They sat still for a moment together in the kitchen, both going over what happened.

"I think that the fact both Robert and I are unharmed and felt unthreatened today when it all happened, we should put this down to a one-off experience and carry on living in this house as normal. We shouldn't worry your parents; they'll only concern themselves and more than likely worry about my mental state. I think this is best kept between us and if anything else is to happen, we'll then inform your Mum and Dad." Ellen suggested, trying to down play the day's events.

She wanted to keep it from Henry and Flo. They'd already been trying to persuade Ellen to return to work once or twice a week whilst they looked after Robert, but she was determined that she would look after her baby at least until he started school.

"Are you sure, sweetheart? I don't want to be worried that you aren't safe here whilst I'm at work. I don't want you to be frightened in your own home. Do you promise that you're OK with this?" Richard asked.

"I promise," Ellen said firmly.

And so it was decided; Robert's visitor would remain a secret, at least for the time being. Perhaps they had convinced themselves that it wouldn't happen again and they were naïve enough to believe that they were safe in that house. A house that had death in its walls and that was coming alive right in front of their eyes.

Chapter Seven

In 1939, the Second World War began and all those who lived in London and other cities around the UK could opt for evacuation. Although thousands of women and predominantly children, were evacuated all over towns and villages in the UK to escape the Blitz, the Camps decided to stay put. That was until things showed no signs of coming to an end and in January 1944, Ellen and Flo agreed to take the boys on the first train to a small village called Overton, Hampshire. Robert was almost four and in December 1942, Ellen gave birth to their second son, Eric. As the boys were so young it was easy to make the process sound like an adventure and, not being aware of the situation, Robert was quite excited.

After several hours of travelling and jumping between stations they finally arrived in the quaint little village of Overton. They had no idea what to expect or where they were would stay but they were happy to be out of the darkness that had fallen over London. The weather was mild for that time of year, with just a cold chill that blew through the air as they jumped off the train. They'd decided they would evacuate at the last minute, so they took little luggage with them so not to overload themselves. Having Eric, who was eighteen months old and Robert, who was almost two and a half, the children were enough to carry alone.

Both Richard and Henry had been called to war almost two years before and had to serve their time protecting their country which meant that poor Ellen and Flo were left unsure of their safety, or even whether they were still alive.

At the station they were given directions and sent to a house which was set far back from the coast, down a small lane called Creaky Coven. The family had no choice but to walk, following the directions of the man at the station. It was only about three miles before they arrived at a large white-bricked cottage which sat back from the road by at least twenty meters. Very different from their town house in the city.

"This is it. What do you think kids?" Flo said to her grandchildren, whilst admiring the elegance of the building in front of her.

The house was full of character, even from the outside, with large white wooden windows, two double chimneys and more foliage covering the brickwork than there was in the gardens; Flo imagined that in the summer, in its full splendour, the house would be absolutely glorious. For a moment she felt envious of those living there whist her family was in the midst of the hustle and bustle of London.

"Come on, let's go inside." Ellen suggested, taking the hand of her eldest son whilst her mother-in-law pushed Eric.

They walked across the front porch as a freezing chill hurried them along.

Just as Ellen reached for the large, gold knocker, the front door was pulled open and stood in front of them was an elderly man, in his eighties at least. He stood no taller than five feet, had a head full of silver-grey hair and a moustache to match.

"Hello," he greeted, "and you must be…?"

"The Camps," Ellen replied, taking a step forward to shake the man's hand. "And who might you be?"

"My name's David Williams. Me and my wife own this house and have opened it to city folk like you during the war" David told them whilst walking them through into the grand entrance hall.

The décor was quite old-fashioned with dark, patterned carpets, clashing drapes, and dark furniture. The walls were left neutral which opened the place up even more than was already apparent and the large, deep mahogany-coloured beams turned this large cottage into a truly spectacular place.

"We, or rather, I, have thirteen guests including you four. I do have some dreadful news to pass on," he said, holding onto Flo's gaze, "My wife passed away three days ago. She had cancer and we knew death was coming for her, nonetheless, it never makes it any easier or any less painful to forget. Unfortunately, with the war taking authority over pretty much everything at the moment, we weren't able to get poor Doris to the hospital; she wouldn't have wanted to

83

take up a bed anyway but due to this, we've had to keep her in the house," David said, dropping his troubled eyes to the ground. "I know it's not ideal but I'm not having her body kept outside, not now, not ever, and as it stands we only have two small rooms left in the house; the room we converted into a bedroom a year or so back which has one small bed inside, and one double room next door. The double room is where Doris is."

The two women never said a word, just looked at each other and then at the children.

"OK," Flo started, "so what you're telling me is that my grandchildren will have to share a room with a corpse?"

David shuffled his feet back and forth, uncomfortably, not knowing how to reply.

"That's correct and, unfortunately, if you don't like it, then I will have to ask you to leave. I mean it's not as though she can hurt them; she's dead!" he exclaimed. "Gathering that you want to stay, here are your keys to room four and five. The only rules I have are that you're home by ten o'clock and that you tidy up after yourself," he told them, now pacing the hallway back and forth. "We all share the kitchen which is straight ahead of you, the lounge which is just in there," he gestured towards the double wooden doors in front of him, "and your rooms are upstairs and to the right. You can't miss them. Now if you need anything, you'll find me in my bedroom which is room number one. Until then, I'm sure you can show yourself about."

With that, he handed Ellen the keys and made his way into the lounge.

The Camps settled in well that afternoon, making acquaintance with the other guests staying at the house. There were two other families, the Jacksons and the Partridges; Juliette Jackson and her two children, Bobby and Ronald and Helen Partridge and her three girls, Rebecca, Julia and Sarah. Everyone seemed friendly enough but there was still the small situation of the dead body in the large bedroom. Ellen had suggested to Flo that they should secretly move her outside or that they all sleep in the smaller room but, as Flo had confirmed, they wouldn't be able to move a rigor-mortis-ridden body out of such a large house without being caught, and a single bed in a room the size of an airing cupboard was too small for two people, let alone four.

Up until seven o'clock, they had avoided entering the double room and had left their unpacked suitcases in the smaller of the rooms whilst they decided what to do.

"We can't let the children sleep in there alone with a corpse, any more than we can't have both children in the box room," Flo said whilst she took the last few sips from her mug. "I suggest," she said whilst raising her hand in imaginary defence against Ellen, "and don't bite my head off before I finish. You sleep in the box room with Eric and I will take the larger room with Robert, and I will also take the bed closest to the body."

The women sat looking at each other. Whilst neither of them had a better suggestion, Ellen was reluctant to agree but had no choice in the matter.

"Then we must go in and make sure the boys aren't going to be able to see the body; we can cover her over or something. I'll go take a look whilst you look after the kids. I'll be back in five minutes and if I'm not, come find me."

Ellen stood up and made her way out of the lounge and into the hallway. She'd never seen a dead body before and didn't really know what to expect. She knew it wouldn't be pleasant but she didn't know how unpleasant. She needed to prepare herself. When she reached the top of the stairs, she turned to face the damned door and reached out towards it with her right hand. It felt icy cold beneath her grip and her instinct was to let go. Reminding herself that it was winter and a cold doorknob was entirely normal, she repeated her actions and this time turned the knob clockwise until the catch released and the door opened.

In front of her was a bare room with two single beds inside that had been pushed together. Initially, she didn't see Mrs Williams and had to step herself into the room before she spotted a deep crimson blanket covering something in the corner of the room. From beneath the blanket, Ellen could see chair legs poking out but because of the height of the blanket, it had clearly been thrown over something. As she felt the sweat trickle down the back of her neck, Ellen made her way slowly over to where the corpse was hiding and slowly drew back the putrid smelling blanket, that smelt similar to rotting beef, and caused her to heave. Turning her head away, she caught sight of a pale white hand that was streaked with thin blue veins, resembling the lines of a dual carriageway on a road map. As she threw her hand over her mouth, Flo came walking into the room.

"Oh my God, are you OK? What's that smell?" she asked, taking two steps back outside the room.

"It's the body; it's hidden underneath that blanket," Ellen said pointing in the direction she'd just been. "We're going to have to wrap it up properly, with two of you in here tonight, it's going to get hot and the heat will only intensify that stench. We need some more sheets. Go get some from Mr Williams, say the boys will be cold without them."

Flo left the room and did as she was asked. They spent the next thirty minutes or so, wrapping the body as tightly as they could whilst holding their breath so as not to choke on the putrid fumes. By nine o'clock, they were all tired out and made their way to bed with the children. Robert, unknowingly, jumped into the bed closest to the body. Flo didn't want to overdramatize the situation, so she didn't say a word as she tucked him in. Secretly, she was pleased she wasn't the one who would have to be just a few feet from a dead old lady, who was rotting away beneath a pile of sheets. Robert was so young that he wouldn't have known what was going on and, even if he did, he wouldn't have understood just how morbid the situation was. It would be a secret the women would keep for as long as they lived, or at least until the boys were old enough to find the funny side.

Chapter Eight

Richard and Henry returned home from war unharmed in 1945 and it wasn't long after that Ellen found out she was pregnant with their third child, Keith. Richard was constantly busy with work in photography. It seemed that once the war was over, people had more interest in saving memories and he was getting enquiries to photograph families, regularly those who had been divided during the war and were now reunited. Ellen was spending more time with Flo, who was a great help with the children who were now aged four, three and Keith who was twelve months. Too young to attend school, the boys took up most of Ellen's time, but now that Flo had given up work, she was happy to take the boys off Ellen's hands twice a week so that she was able to lunch with friends, shop and attend a tapestry class which she had recently taken up. Life was good. It seemed a long time ago that Ellen had experienced anything untoward in their home. As agreed, they never spoke of what happened, nor did they share the experience with anyone, including Flo and Henry. They thought that by sweeping it under the carpet, they wouldn't upset anyone or encourage anything to happen again. It was in the past and now all they wanted was to concentrate on a bright, happy future.

It was a beautiful July afternoon and Ellen had arranged to meet with her best friends, Julie and Helen, for lunch. Flo had agreed to look after the children as Richard was working. Although Ellen loved her boys, she did tend to look forward to her days off. It allowed her to remember who she was in those years before motherhood; in fact her best friends were there the night that she met Richard and she partly had them to thank for their introduction.

Today they were heading to Julie's house for sandwiches and cake, giving them a chance to catch up. Julie had been married to Peter for two years and they had been trying for a child ever since he returned home from fighting in the war but she hadn't yet fallen pregnant. Helen was still single. She wasn't keen on the idea of settling down and preferred a life full of surprises, and change and she didn't associate marriage with this. Ellen often felt sorry for her friend not having the commitment and stability that both Julie and herself had in their marriage and she pitied her friend Julie as she had been so lucky to be blessed with three healthy, beautiful boys whilst she was struggling to fall pregnant with her first. She loved meeting up with them both and hearing about their lives and how they were all growing up but she didn't like to discuss herself too much, as she always felt as if she was bragging.

"I hear Richard's doing well with his photography. I spoke to Vera last week and she told me that she was booking him to photograph her and her family. Word is spreading and he is becoming quite the talk of the town. You may be able to get a place of your own if his success continues?" Helen asked but in such a way that she wasn't expecting an honest response. However Ellen was happy to elaborate.

"Yes he's doing very well but that's not to say that he isn't working long hours and I'm not seeing him less because he isn't home as much as he'd like to be, you know. If I'm honest, whilst the idea of getting our own place seems like a dream on the one hand, on the other we would have a lot of things we would lose out on. We have an in-house babysitter, financial stability, help around the house and I also enjoy the company if I'm honest. I love Flo and Henry and I'm not sure we'd want to move out even if we could."

Although Ellen's reply sounded prompted, it wasn't. She spoke from the heart and although neither she nor Richard had ever brought it up, she knew that Richard felt the same. Although nothing alarming had happened at Poultney Road for some years, they still felt responsible for what had happened and Ellen knew that if they did move out, it would be their responsibility to tell Flo and Harry and she didn't want to be in that position.

"I can understand that, it must be hard looking after three boys by yourself," Julie answered. Ellen was unsure whether or not the comment had double meaning. She knew that Julie was envious of her life so she decided not to bite. She knew how hard Richard was working and that, in fact, she loved every minute she spent with her boys. She knew that, really, she was content in her own life and didn't need the envy of her friends to appreciate what she had.

She kissed her friends goodbye late afternoon on that glorious day and headed home at about five o'clock, in time to make dinner for her family. She walked home thinking about the day's events and her friend's stories she'd been told. Although they were all getting older, they never failed to enjoy one another's company. As Ellen turned the corner onto Poultney Road, she could see people out of their homes and on the pavements looking over at number 106 and as she picked up her pace and grew closer to the crowd she saw that two police cars were parked outside her house. Her stomach turned as the penny dropped that the police were inside her home. She ran to the front porch and leaped up the steps to the front door which was still slightly open.

"Flo? Henry? Where are you? What's going on?" Ellen screamed as she ran through the hall to the kitchen where she laid eyes on Robert.

"Mummy, Mummy!" the small boy cried out as he ran towards her with open arms. As she lifted her son up, Flo stood from the table and stepped towards her daughter-in-law.

"Please stay calm, the police are here as a precaution. We heard Robert talking to himself earlier when he was playing in the lounge. We put it down to his imagination until we heard him struggle and start to scream."

As Flo continued to speak, Ellen caught sight of a large bruise on the side of Roberts head.

"What the hell is that?" Ellen yelled.

"That was what I was getting to. We ran straight into him but there was no one there but he was screaming about someone wearing a white robe. He's been saying things like it ever since. Henry ran out of the house of course, but he couldn't see anyone. We think that maybe we scared them off but they must have been quick and we can't work out how they got in or out of the house. All the doors were locked from the inside," Flo explained. "We took him straight to the police station and they've come back here to check that everything's in order."

"Good evening, Mrs Camp, my name is PC Noland and I'd just like to ask you a few questions."

The policeman worked his way through a set of questions, asking about where she had spent her afternoon, who she was with and how long she was out of the house. She answered every question with ease and was soon walking the policeman out of her house.

"Any more problems at all, just make your way back down to the station, but I'm sure whoever done this is long gone." PC Noland assured her as he turned to leave and as he did, Ellen could see Richard making his way up the road.

He threw his bike to the floor and jumped up the three steps into the hall.

"What's going on? Was that the police? Is everything OK?"

Ellen could sense that he was panicking and so suggested that they went for a walk so she could explain what had happened without the children overhearing.

"But how could anyone get in, like Mum and Dad said, the house was locked from the inside. It's impossible," Richard said, confused and unable to comfort his wife with reassuring words when he didn't have any. "None of it makes any sense. How had Robert got a bruise on his head? Has anyone asked him how it happened or what the intruder looked like?"

"Yes," Ellen replied, "I did. He says it was a lady dressed in white with long black hair." They both stared at each other without saying a word; a minute of utter silence when neither one of them managed to find their voice.

"Do you think it could be her? The woman I saw standing over Robert's cot?" Ellen asked. "It could be, Richard, it scares me. What are we going to do?"

It wasn't a rhetorical question, but Richard was unable to reply. He just stood like an empty shell staring into the sky, reaching for answers, for a way out of the situation he and his family were in.

"I don't know Ellen. Maybe Mum was right and someone broke in, maybe Dad left the back door open and they jumped the fence at the station. Let's try to believe that, we have to." Richard said as he wrapped his jacket over his wife's bare shoulders. "Come on, let's go home and take little Robert's mind off of it, he must have been so frightened."

They walked back to number 106 without saying a word, both speechless, trying to think of a logical explanation for the day's events. Once home, they told both Flo and Henry not to discuss what had happened in front of the children so that, hopefully, Robert would forget with time. They enjoyed dinner, which Flo had surprised them with and then finished off with a game of hide and seek.

"You seek, I'll hide, please Mummy, can I?" Robert whined.

"OK, I'll count to 106, slowly, so you have a chance to find a good hiding space. I'll start counting... now!" and with that Robert ran out of the kitchen and up the stairs.

He ran into the back bedroom and slammed the door behind him. It was a dark room and Robert was pretty certain that he wouldn't be found if he hid underneath the small pull-down bed. He bent down onto his tiny knees and wriggled and pulled his way underneath, ensuring that every part of him was tucked under. He lay there for a while, scrunched into a foetal position, when he suddenly heard footsteps. It was too dark to see but it sounded as though they were coming from the other side of the room.

How could Mummy have got in without me seeing? Robert thought as he tightened his position slightly. Perhaps it's Daddy coming to hide with me; but the door is still closed.

He wasn't sure what to think, but decided to sit tight. As he peered out from underneath the bed, his eyes were desperately trying to focus on his surroundings, clasping onto every outline they managed to recognise. Then he heard the footsteps again, closer this time and quicker; whoever it was moved quickly and seemed to be getting closer to where he was hiding. Then they stopped. Nothing but utter silence; he couldn't even hear the sound of his family who were just outside the room. Imperceptibly, the temperature of the room had plummeted and, only because of the intense darkness, Robert was unable to see the frosty breath coming from his humid mouth as he breathed rapidly, his heartbeat racing. He sat silently, listening to the sound of his breathing. In, out. In, out. He held on to his breath for a moment but the breathing continued. It wasn't his breath he was listening to. He turned his head to his shoulder, slowly, and there beside him, laid in an identical position, was a small boy with unwashed red hair and dirty clothes. As Robert opened his mouth to scream, the young boy beside him raised his finger to his lips and urged his silence. Robert was unable to find his voice or his feet as he clambered his way out from under the bed and, as his hands gripped and turned the door handle, he let rip with an almighty scream.

"MUMMY!" he yelled, but at the same time he could hear his mother screaming from downstairs.

He ran as fast as his little legs would carry him and when he reached the bottom of the stairs he was unable to believe what he saw. In front of him was the bedroom that his brother Eric shared with his younger brother Keith. In the doorway stood his parents and grandparents and in the middle of the room sat Eric who was staring transfixed on Keith's cot in which he was laying as still as a corpse. Above Keith's cot flew a toy aeroplane, made from plastic, finished in a navy blue. It was Robert's favourite toy, he recognised it right away. He played for hours flying it around the room but, unlike now, he would have to lift it manually to make it move; the toy contained no motor or batteries so it was impossible for it to move of its own accord, let alone fly by itself. They all watched in disbelief as it glided effortlessly in a circular motion above Keith's cot. None of the family moved, they all just stood in silence, watching the impossible.

"Amazing." Henry spoke. "How is this happening?"

As the words came out of his mouth, there was a sudden chill which swept past the hallway where they were standing and as Ellen turned with the breeze, they were all scared out of their wits as the door to the back-room upstairs slammed shut, crashing the model plane to the ground.

*****

It was now undeniable that something inexplicable was happening to the Camp family. That something they had all been a part of, all witnessed, was really happening and none

97

of them were able to explain it. It was apparent that there was something in the house and, whatever it was, was targeting the children. The woman in white whom Ellen had seen watching over Robert when he was a baby, possibly the same entity that had attacked him that afternoon, a child that showed himself to Robert also, and now all of the family had been witness to a non-motorised children's toy flying by itself. After explaining everything to Flo and Henry, the family had to consider their future, living in the house; a way for them to coexist with the spirits that were haunting the house. Richard decided that the best place to start was by visiting the library to do some research on the area, and also on ghosts and the afterlife. It was Friday afternoon and he'd only had one shoot that morning, a woman who wanted adorning photos of her three-month-old baby. He was finished by two o'clock so he had the time to stop on his way home to do some research. Making his way into the library they stopped him and made him fill in some forms, declaring his name and address and in return, handed him a library card. He headed into the small but well-resourced library; there must have been more than a thousand books in there. He passed the fiction area, Jane Ayre, Wuthering Heights, until he saw, in the corner, boxes full of newspaper clippings entitled Local History. He lifted a lid and started rummaging his way through page after page of newspaper stories. Local fires, missing people, war news, but nothing about Poultney Road. Richard lost himself in the stories when all of a sudden the room darkened.

"Mr Camp? Are you still in here?" a woman asked peering round from the corner of the front desk. "We close in five minutes, it's almost six o'clock."

He couldn't believe it, he'd been in there for almost four hours and, in that time, hadn't found a single thing that could lead him to an explanation of what was happening to his family.

"I won't be a minute. Do you have any books on the supernatural? About ghosts and things like that?" Richard asked.

"We don't have much," the woman eyed him suspiciously through the narrow spectacles resting on the tip of her nose. "We did have a book come in a few weeks ago called Do We Really Cross Over, it should be in the non-fiction section under D. Let me know if you have any problems finding it."

Richard made his way quickly over to the area she pointed out and managed to find the book with ease. He grabbed it off the shelf and ran over to the counter.

"Thank you for waiting, I completely lost myself in history, so many interesting stories and people. I could have stayed in here reading all night. This should occupy me this evening, though. Thank you."

The woman paused momentarily and asked, "If you don't mind me asking, was there something you were looking for? Only we don't have many people lose themselves in old newspaper clippings and then leave with a book about ghosts. I'm intrigued."

"So am I," Richard answered before exchanging a smile and leaving.

*****

By the time he got home, it was past seven o'clock and he was late for dinner.

"Where have you been, Richard, we've been worried sick. The boys were desperate for you to read to them before bed but it got too late so they've gone to sleep worried and, without saying goodnight," Ellen complained.

"I'm sorry sweetheart, I got caught up. I'll go and look in on them now. What's for dinner, I'm starving," Richard replied and took off down the hall with the book still hidden under his arm.

He first made his way into his two youngest boy's room, creeping in through the bedroom door; he tried to silence the handle as he pushed it down and made his way in. Both boys were asleep so he kissed them both on the forehead and made his way back to the corridor and to his eldest son's room. He crept in but had a feeling that he would be asleep and he was right. He was lying under his blanket, dreaming peacefully; it was hard to imagine the terrors of the day before. Whilst he thought about the bruise on Robert's head and the flying toy, he pulled the book from under his arm and slid down the side of Robert's bed onto the floor where he sat whilst he read the first few pages. It talked about dying and what happens to the soul; that our bodies are a shell concealing the soul and is what holds on to all of our thoughts and memories and are what we take when we pass over, leaving our shell on earth to waste away. To heaven go Christians, to hell for all evil or those who commit offences; or, there is another place where souls go that are confused, and perhaps murdered, or, are suicide victims; people who won't accept that they're dead. These souls are trapped between heaven and earth and can often live in parallel to us, our lives intertwining, torture for them as they are so close but unable to communicate but, sometimes, there is a way that they can be seen, they can create havoc among the living and appear to us.

Richard read every word, taking everything in as he had no experience or knowledge of anything supernatural besides his own experience. He was unsure whether or not to believe the concepts within the book and decided that perhaps he had to formulate his own ideas, and that would mean delving deeper.

"Richard, dinner's ready," Ellen's voice called down the hallway.

"I'm coming," Richard replied as he slipped the book under his son's bed and softly kissed him goodnight.

Chapter Nine

The next day was Sunday and Richard had arranged a darts competition with his friends at the Old Bell. It was something he arranged once a month that gave him time to kick back and relax. Although he adored his family, it was nice to spend a couple of hours at the pub with his friends. It was almost six o'clock so he kissed his wife and children goodbye and promised to be home before eleven. He grabbed his jacket, stepped out the front door and ran across the road to the pub, trying to get out of the rain as quickly as he could. The weather had taken a turn for the worse that morning but it didn't stop him wanting to have a boys' night. When he entered, his friends had a beer waiting for him.

"Richard, where have you been, your beer's getting warm," Jerry mocked. "Come on, son, we've been waiting to kick your arse."

"Thanks for this, Jerry," Richard said as he raised his glass. "Here's to winning all your money," he teased.

The men began to play, whilst chatting about everyday things. They'd been playing for almost an hour and had the attention of many of the other customers. They liked to place bets on who would win; it had become quite a popular event. When everyone was in the swing of the competition, the lights behind the bar began to flicker.

"Must be that damn generator," John cursed. "Keeps bloody wiping out." As the words came out of his mouth, so the power went completely.

"Spooky. I think it's the old ghosts playing about with your electrics," Martin joked.

Martin was a good-looking chap with sleek dark hair he always combed to the left, with dark brown eyes to match. He had always been a hit with the ladies as his looks complemented his confident personality. He was the cockiest of the group, thought of himself as a bit of a Jack-the-lad as he was the only one still single and living the bachelor life.

"Shut up, Martin, you'll scare off all my punters! Everyone keep calm, I'll go downstairs and get the problem fixed. I won't be two seconds," John assured as he ran through the back doors and down the stairs to the cellar.

"What a pain, I was onto a winner here tonight. Shall we count up and postpone until next week?" Jerry asked.

"We can do. Here, Jerry, what was that you were saying about old ghosts? You don't think this place is haunted, do you?" Richard asked, trying not to sound too melodramatic.

"I was just kidding but it wouldn't surprise me, an old place like this. It must have history. Why the sudden interest?" Jerry asked.

Richard didn't answer for a moment. He didn't know whether or not he should open up to his friends, or would they think he was crazy? He didn't have much to lose and at that moment he would take advice from anyone who was willing to give it.

"I think our house is haunted." It came out as easily as if he had said I'm having stew for dinner. "I've known it for a few years now but have never said anything to anyone. I thought I was going crazy but recently, Ellen, Mum and Dad have all witnessed it for themselves. I know I'm not crazy but I don't know what I can do about it. I don't care if you think I'm mad but, if you don't, then I think I might need your help."

They all just sat in silence for a moment, looking at Richard but with their thoughts elsewhere. Obviously an issue such as this wasn't often brought up and none of them knew how to react.

"Well, I don't think any of us expected that," Martin said. "What are you going to do about it?"

"I don't know, that's why I'm telling you. What would you do?" Richard asked with sincerity.

"You could do a Ouija board?" Jerry suggested. "Or a séance?"

"Ellen and I have tried a Ouija, a couple of years ago and although it did work, I'm not sure it had the outcome we wanted, even though at the time we thought it did. What's a séance? Tell me more."

"Don't get me wrong, I've never tried one myself but I know some friends who did. I think they were just messing about and again, I'm not sure how successful it was but it could be worth a try. You need to get a few people together who are believers and be prepared to host the séance yourself. You get everyone to stand round in a circle and try to speak to the spirits, or whatever it is you want to call them. Ask them questions, see what they want. Like I say, I'm not saying it'll work, but it could be worth a shot," Jerry finished.

"Would you lot be prepared to help?" Richard pleaded.

"So long as there's a beer in it for us," Martin replied just as the lights came back on.

*****

Richard got together a small group of friends, Martin, Jerry, John, and Jack and, although he had no idea what to expect, he was keen to get to the bottom of whatever was haunting his house. He thought too about the possibility that they may get in touch with his childhood friend, and of the potential consequences of this but he was prepared to try anything, especially if it could help his friend rest in peace. They decided to do it on an evening when the rest of Richard's family were out. Although he wasn't sure of how successful it would be, Richard didn't want to put any of his family, especially his children, at risk. Over the past week, he had done a fair bit of research and read about all types of outcomes, from possession to apparitions and even spontaneous combustion. He also read that many attempts to contact the dead were unsuccessful but, after what he and his family had experienced, he was feeling positive. He ensured that all of his friends were alcohol-free so that they were open to channelling. Although he wasn't sure of anything, all he did know was that he wanted to do everything he could to encourage the séance to work.

He'd moved a table into the front spare bedroom on the second floor. It was one of the larger rooms in the house and perfect for holding such meetings. He emptied the room, with a little help from his dad. This was suggested in one of the books; it made it less likely that any interfering incidents could be confused with paranormal activity. An empty space made it harder for any spoofs to occur.

Everyone arrived on time as Richard said goodbye to his family as they left to visit friends. He welcomed everyone into his home and sat them down in the lounge to go through the procedure.

"OK, so you all know I'm not an expert at this kind of thing but I've done a fair bit of research so that I have an idea of what to do and what to expect. Can you all ensure me that you've not drank any alcohol today?" Richard asked.

Everyone looked at him blankly.

"It's important no one's drank. It can prevent it from working and would be a waste of everyone's time. I know what you lot are like. You're bloody alcoholics!" he joked.

The five men made their way upstairs, none of them knowing what to expect and half-expecting nothing to happen. None of them had previously experienced anything supernatural but neither did they have a reason to be sceptical. They all entered the front bedroom and positioned themselves in a circle.

"Where do you want us, Dick?" Dick was the diminutive his friends had developed over the past couple of months. No particular reason why. "Just in a circle? Want us to hold hands?" Martin asked.

"I think that's the way, yes Martin. I'm going to turn the lights out and when I do, I want us all to hold hands, one palm facing up and the other facing down. Then just follow my commands." Richard said.

"Yes, sir," Martin joked.

Richard grinned as he made his way over to the light switch; he turned to look at his friends. "Are you ready for this?" he asked.

"Ready as we'll ever be," Jerry replied as the lights went out.

Richard joined his friends back in the middle of the room and they formed a circle, palms alternating at Richard's request. The room was very dark with only a small amount of natural light from the full moon entering through the large bay window. They stood, awkward for a moment, in silence and waiting for their first instruction. Richard was the most nervous of them all; nervous that nothing would happen and that he would be the laughing stock of his friends and, worse still, nervous that something would happen and he wouldn't know what to do and the situation would get out of hand.

"OK you're going to have to bear with me as I'm new to this," he laughed awkwardly. "If we can all close our eyes and empty our minds. Try not to think of anything in particular, but leave your mind open and allow it to wander freely," he requested. "I ask any spirits of those in this room with us, to come forward and let us know who you are. If anyone is there, give us a sign."

The five men stood in silence, Martin fidgeting nervously as they embraced their surroundings.

"If anyone is there, please make yourself present. We don't mean you any harm, we are simply trying to help..."

Richard's sentence was cut short by a strange noise coming from the hallway behind the closed door.

"Did you hear that?" Martin whispered. "Did anyone else hear that?"

"Of course we did Martin, we all did," Jerry answered.

As they stood together anxiously in the dark room, they all reached out to whatever they had heard on the other side of the door, terrified but all desperately hoping that they would hear it again.

"If that was you and you are in the room with us, or elsewhere in the house, please do what you just did again." Richard commanded.

Nothing. Just the ticking of the old grandfather clock that sat high on the wall beside the door. All eager to encourage whatever it was Richard was trying to contact, Jack, a large, stocky man whom everyone respected for his stern views and strong voice, spoke out.

"Please, if there is anyone there who is trying to communicate with Richard or any one of us, please come forward and let yourself be known."

They stood still for almost ten minutes and what seemed like an eternity, without so much as a sound.

"Come on, Dick, maybe it's just not their time tonight. Perhaps if we tried another time then ..." Martin trailed off. "Bloody hell," he said as he looked over towards the closed bedroom door. "Am I the only one seeing this?"

The men all turned to face the door and, to their astonishment, it was slowly but quite clearly opening. None of them could speak, they all just watched as the door moved, all questioning the evidence of their own eyes.

"It's not possible." Martin said.

"Well it is because we can all see this, right?" Jerry asked. All of the men mumbled a resounding yes.

"Who are you? We bring no harm to you and we ask for you to do the same," Richard spoke as the door was pushed fully open. "Harry, is that you?" he asked.

The door stopped, opened wide with the empty landing in full view. The men were still, the house was silent and there was no sign of anyone or anything that had opened the door.

"Harry, I'm so sorry for that day. I'm so sorry you died. Please forgive me," Richard pleaded, and with a sudden and almighty strength the door was thrown closed, knocking the ticking clock from its place on the wall.

All of the men stood still and, for a moment, none of them spoke. They all waited as if something was going to happen, jump out at them perhaps. Nothing did happen, and they waited for almost five minutes before deciding to break the circle. It's important not to break a chain when doing a séance as often the energy or spirits are connected through those involved with the séance, and that energy is built up in the centre of the circle. By breaking the chain early, a spirit can be lost in limbo, unable to return to its comfort zone. Richard okayed the breaking of the chain but, as the men lowered their hands, none of them moved. They all stood in the darkness.

"Do you think whatever it is, is waiting out there for us?" Jack asked. "I'm not sure I want to leave the room if I'm honest."

"I'll go," Richard volunteered.

As he approached the door he could see that there was a mark on the inside, yet he was unable to make out exactly what it was. He reached for the light switch, flicked it, but they remained in darkness.

"Damn!" he cursed.

Closer to the door he could see that the dark, black mark was in the shape of a handprint; a large, spread handprint.

"Not possible," he concluded but as his brain processed the image, he realised that if the handprint was on the inside, then the door was slammed shut from a force within the room. This meant that Jack needn't have worried about leaving the room in fear of what was awaiting them outside; because whatever it was that had forced the door closed, was in fact inside the room with them. Richard quickly turned towards his friends to calmly explain the situation but, as he did, he was distracted by a shadowed silhouette standing in the far corner of the room. Although there were no lights on, his eyes had adjusted slightly to the dark.

112

"Richard, what is it? What's the matter?" John asked.

Richard didn't reply, his eyes frozen on the dark figure stood behind his friends.

"It can't be."

He tried to convince himself but, as he got closer to his friends and nearer to whatever it was that stood before him, he recognised the long black coat and hidden face. It was the same man that he saw the day his friend died. The man that had drawn his attention and distracted him from the route he took with his dear friend. The man in black.

"Don't panic, boys, but we aren't alone. Can you slowly turn to face the far right corner of the room and tell me what you see?"

Just as he asked, the men apprehensively turned in the direction that Richard was facing and, one-by-one, they gasped in horror as each of them could see the apparition, or ghost, or whatever it was.

"It's a man, Dick, a man dressed in black. Am I right? Is this what everyone else sees?" Jack questioned. No one answered. "Answer me, do you all see the same?" Jack began to panic.

"Yes, Jack, we do and I want to get out of here," John proclaimed but, before he found his footing, there was a loud crash from the hallway which made them all jump out their skins and, as they did, so the lights came back on. Of course, during all of this, they lost sight of the man dressed in black and, when they looked back, they found themselves alone in the room.

"What the hell was that? We all saw it, right?" Martin questioned.

"We all saw it, Martin," Jerry confirmed. "I think we deserve a drink. Richard, you game?"

Richard gave Martin a nod as they all made their way swiftly out of the bedroom and downstairs whilst Richard stayed behind, pulling Jerry back with him.

"Jerry, look at this." Richard showed him the handprint on the door. "This wasn't here before, it must have been made from whoever ... whatever slammed shut this door. It was closed from the inside of the room."

Jerry eyed his friend carefully. "Do you think it was him? The man in black?"

"I don't know but if it was and he can leave a handprint on a solid wooden door, what could he do to my family?"

The two men left the room in silence, neither one of them knowing what to say. The evening had been successful, but what on earth would Richard tell his family without scaring the living hell out of them?

*****

The men all made their way over to the Old Bell in as little time as possible, none of them wanting to stay a minute longer in number 106. Whilst his friends sat themselves at the table furthest from the bar and out of earshot of other punters, Richard ordered five pints of IPA. As he took their drinks over to the table, he noted that his friends quit their conversation as soon as he approached.

"You don't have to stop talking on my account, I know what we just witnessed and I know that it's not something that can go without discussion." Richard paused. "I'll start you off. I'm terrified of going home, I have no idea what to say happened to my family and whether or not I can honestly tell them that they're safe living there."

The men all sat in silence.

"It's not a secret, Richard, what just happened has scared us all and we are worried for you and your family," Jerry explained. "Obviously, we want to support you as much as possible but we must consider our own families and the safety of them. How do we know that whatever we contacted tonight won't follow us home? How can we know that we are safe? It was no one's imagination, we all saw a man in the room with us. A man in black. How do we know that he hasn't come for one of us. It has really worried us," Jerry said with sincerity. "We want to help you Richard, but I think that perhaps you need help from someone who knows what they're doing."

"Thanks for your support chaps, I never expected tonight to end the way it did. I thought we would be lucky to contact anything, let alone see someone or something standing in front of us. I'm as much shocked as you are and I don't blame you for feeling the way you do, but you must understand that I can't just leave it there. I have a family to look after and my number one priority is their safety. In fact I'm going to leave you now and go home to them and try to explain what happened this evening. I would prefer it if you kept what happened to yourselves for now, at least until I know where to go from here," Richard requested as he stood from the table and pulled on his raincoat. "Thanks once again, I can only apologise that it's left you with unanswered questions. I'll see you on Sunday as usual to win all your money."

Richard left without waiting for a response from his friends. There was little any one of them could say. He pushed open the heavy pub front door and made his way across the street. It was almost ten o'clock and it was dark with only the light from the stars and moon reflecting down on his passage home. It was a mild evening but there was a strong breeze which left a chill in the air. It was a short walk but Richard took it slow. He wanted to have the story clear in his mind before he made it home. He needed to be confident when telling his family of the night's events. He thought for a while and decided that he would perhaps miss out the part where they were accompanied by what he believed was the omen that had followed him from his childhood. He looked both ways before crossing, when he suddenly heard footsteps behind him.

"Richard, wait," his friend Jerry called out after him. "Richard, I want to speak to you."

The two men met in the middle of the road.

"Tonight terrified me, Richard, I'm not going to lie but, I must admit, curiosity has got the better of me. You know that I lost my mum last year and I miss her deeply. I would love to think that she is somewhere close to me, able to see me. I would be happy to attend again at one of your sittings, should you do one," Jerry explained.

"I don't know what I'm going to do just yet. I must get home to my family; they'll be waiting and keen to know what happened. I just don't know what to tell them. I'll have a think and let you know what I intend to do from here when I see you on Sunday." Richard replied.

"OK," said Jerry. Night."

The two men parted and, as Richard made his way across the road, he noticed that all of the downstairs lights were on in number 106. Ellen must be putting the children to bed as it was well past their usual bedtime and, no doubt, his mum would be making them all a cup of cocoa. He had decided to tell them only of the noises and sounds that they heard. Nothing about the physical manifestations they had witnessed as it would only worry them all. As he turned the key to his family home, he could have sworn that he saw someone pull the curtains of the window in the front of the house upstairs, but he could only pray that it had been his imagination.

Chapter Ten

As arranged, Richard saw his friends the next Sunday and they played darts as usual. None of the men mentioned what had happened during the séance at number 106 earlier that week; they just played, chatted and had a few drinks just as though nothing had happened. Richard had, however, given the entire situation a great deal of thought, including what he wanted to do next. He had discussed what had happened that night in some depth with Ellen and they were both in agreement that they needed to take further action. Richard remembered that his friend Jerry had mentioned an acquaintance who knew about Ouija boards and séances so he decided he would find out more about this contact and get in touch with them. When they finished playing Richard spoke on the quiet to Jerry and got the number of his friend, Benjamin, in whom Richard intended to place his trust.

Benjamin lived just a few stops away by train, in Bethnal Green, and so on his way home from work the following Wednesday, Richard decided to cut his losses and take the early stop and visit Benjamin and see if he was home. He made fast time and was in Bethnal Green by five o'clock, jumped off the train and picked up his pace to the address that Jerry had given him. When he arrived, he saw that the small bungalow the address had bought him to, had the most beautiful garden he had ever seen. He walked along the small pebbled path to the wooden front door, took a deep breath and knocked hard. He was anxious about this meeting, primarily because Benjamin wasn't expecting him and secondly because he didn't know what kind of response he was going to get or what advice he was going to receive. Pretty soon, the door opened and an elderly lady stood in the frame.

"Can I help you?" the grey-haired woman asked.

She must have been in her late seventies and although she clearly looked after her appearance, her age could be seen behind her eyes.

"Yes, I hope you can. I'm looking for Benjamin. My friend Jerry Tyler has put me in touch with him," Richard explained.

"That would be my husband. Come on in."

Richard was taken aback by the lady's friendliness. It can't have happened often that a man turned up on your doorstep asking to speak with your husband; or perhaps it did with this family. He walked into her home and noted that it was immaculately kept; everything seemed to have its place. Richard introduced himself and learned that this welcoming lady's name was Rose.

"I'm sorry to intrude on you like this, it's just I really need your husband's advice on a matter that exceeds my own knowledge and experience. Is your husband home?" Richard questioned.

"Yes, please take a seat and I'll go fetch him for you. Would you like a drink?" Rose asked.

"No, thank you, I'm fine and don't mean to keep you long," he replied as Rose smiled and exited the room.

Whilst alone he sat thinking about the recent events which had unfolded in his home and he wondered why it was that his family appeared to be the target of something so sinister. It did cross his mind that it wasn't in fact his family that was being beleaguered, that actually it was him.

"Good evening, Richard, my wife says that you are here to see me?"

A tall man walked into the room. He had a head thick of silver-grey hair and a beard to match. He was just as welcoming as his wife and Richard didn't find it difficult opening up to him. He began by telling Benjamin about his childhood and the tragedy that took place. He went on to explain that he believed that his friend, Harry, had visited him on several occasions throughout his life and that Richard felt that he was trying to tell him something, or perhaps blamed him for his death. He explained how his children were now involved in the hauntings and that was what concerned him most. He lastly reiterated what had happened with his friends the week before.

"And I guess that brings us up to date. It was my friend, Jerry, who put me in touch with you. I hope you don't mind, he said that you have some experience with this kind of thing?"

Benjamin sat for a   moment.

"I do have personal experience but I'm no expert. I can advise you on my previous experiences and knowledge but don't by any means think that my suggestions are solutions, they are simply a way in which I would deal with the situation, should I be in your shoes. Many years ago I messed about with a Ouija board. It was my friend's idea and it was only meant as a bit of fun but unfortunately it worked. Not in a million years did we think it would, we were just kids messing about, bored and wanting something to do. I remember it as if it were yesterday, it was after school on our way home, we stopped in the woods that took us to Albert Street, not far from here. My intentions were to smoke my first cigarette which my closest friend Peter had taken from his dad's stash but when we settled down, it seemed that he had an entirely different agenda and pulled out an old Ouija board he'd found in his parents' attic." Benjamin went on, "We didn't know what to expect and definitely didn't imagine it to work like it did. It took a while for anything to happen but soon enough, the planchette began to move. We asked the board several questions, like its sex and age and silly stuff like that and, to be perfectly honest, I just thought it was one of the other kids messing about. It wasn't until we asked what its name was that it took a serious turn. It spelt out Peter's brother's name. Peter sat quiet and calculated that the age and sex would both coincide with his brother. I remember Peter asking,

"If this is my brother, Alec, then tell me how you are talking through this, you left school before I did today. Where are you?

"Peter asked, 'where are you?'

"It only took the board seconds to respond and spell out B.E.S.I.D.E.Y.O.U. Peter got up like he'd been shot in the buttocks. It was the following day at school, when Peter never showed up, that we all discovered his brother Alec had been killed on his way home. It was an accident not that dissimilar to your friend, Harry. We were all pretty shook up but it left me intrigued as to how the Ouija board had worked and how I could use it to help people."

"Are you sure you don't want that drink, Richard?" Rose asked.

"I think I will you know and perhaps you should make it a double." Richard replied.

Benjamin continued. "The day when we were in the woods, Peter had been in such a hurry to get home that he forgot to take his board so, without the others noticing, I sneaked it into my bag. Peter never asked us its whereabouts; he never mentioned that day again. It would seem that's how many people cope with such a situation, one they can't explain. They ignore it and pretend it never happened, that way they can go back to their normal lives and not have to think about anything else that may exist. But I couldn't do that. I hid the board under my bed and decided to do some research. To be honest with you, the books I read back then aren't much different to the stuff in the libraries today. It's all people's ideas and interpretations. I haven't come across a single book that comes from experience or proven knowledge besides the Bible, so I decided to throw the books out and let the board do the talking. I would use the board by myself to begin with and at first nothing would happen. I'd sit for hours trying to speak to it and nothing came through but then I got good at it. Patience is a virtue and it paid off. I was only a child and didn't really know what I was doing but now, sixty years later, I have a rough idea."

Rose walked in with Richard's drink, which couldn't have come at a better time.

"Thanks, Rose. I think I'm going to need this," Richard said whilst taking in a deep mouthful of whisky, "I love this stuff. Please continue, Benjamin."

"I was only going to move onto your situation that you're in now. I'm no professional but I do have knowledge. Please remember this is only my opinion. I think that using Ouija boards and participating in séances allows you to connect with those that have passed; people who have died but whose souls cannot rest. Whether they died suddenly in an accident or some other way that was unexpected that has caused their souls to remain here on earth, not understanding what has happened, these souls I would spend forever trying to help, to encourage them to be able to rest in peace. Then there are other souls that are not worth saving. There is a divide in spirits or ghosts that you can contact. The lost souls like the ones I just described and evil ones, people who cannot rest because their souls are too wicked. I would suggest that your friend Harry isn't able to rest because he was taken suddenly, and his spirit wasn't able to adjust. By doing a séance or Ouija board it's going to put you in touch with him because he is already connected to your past. This man in black, however, is something that you should be more concerned with," Benjamin said without hesitation, "He has connected to you as a child, it would seem that, for whatever reason, he keeps appearing to you and your family. A séance or Ouija could help the situation or it could make it worse. It seems that over the years he has kept his distance, but messing with something you don't entirely understand could allow him to get closer. Be curious but just be careful."

Richard sat in silence for a moment.

"Everything you've said makes sense, Benjamin, and it's really helped talking to someone who doesn't think I'm crazy. I wish I could leave alone whatever it is that's haunting my family, but I can't, not when it's involving my wife and kids. I have been thinking long and hard about the best possible solution and I've decided to try to get together a group on a regular basis and try to contact whatever is in my house and see if somehow, we can get rid of it. Would you …"

Before Richard could finish asking the question, Benjamin had already replied, "No. Thank you for asking but my days of messing about with the dead are well and truly passed. I don't doubt that before too long, someone will be trying to contact me," he said with humour.

Richard finished his drink, thanked Rose for her hospitality and Benjamin for his advice.

"Thanks again, Benjamin, speaking with you has clarified a few things I had wandering around in my head," Richard said whilst making his way to the door.

"No problem, Richard, it was nice meeting you and should you ever need my help further, please don't hesitate to get in touch," Benjamin said,

As Richard turned to leave, he felt Benjamin grab hold of his arm.

"Son, be careful, I couldn't say much in front of Rose but I don't think the man in black that you keep seeing is good news. When doing a séance, have a strong chain and never let anyone break it before exiting. If you do, you could be stuck with him or whatever else you contact. Remember, it's not a game, it's serious and sometimes you don't know how serious until it's too late. Good luck and take care." Benjamin closed the door without giving Richard time to respond.

With a head full of new information, he decided to stop off at the Old Bell before heading home.

Chapter Eleven

A week passed and Richard used the time productively. He'd been as vague as he could to his family about his meeting with Benjamin, and had them on a need-to-know basis. Ellen was a little more clued up but his parents and children didn't know any details that they didn't have to. He'd been speaking to friends of friends, trying to get word out that he would be hosting private séances at his home. Several people had been in touch via Jerry or John or one of his other friends, and in total, he had collected the names and addresses of nine people, whom he would visit and discuss the plan of his upcoming sessions.

He already knew Jerry, who wanted to be involved with the Ouija boards and séances since his last experience at number 106 and he spread the word onto three of his friends, Margaret and Paul Liming and Stephen Pillar, none of whom had previous experience but had loved ones who had passed over that they were keen to contact. Although John didn't want to attend anymore of Richard's meetings, he had told a couple of his friends, Mabel and Phillip Turner and their friends, Bessie and Pete Beaton who he thought might be interested in getting involved and they were. There was one other person who had contacted Richard directly, and turned up at his home one evening unprompted. His name was Frank Brately, a preacher who lived in the area and had heard about Richard's meetings through his brother.

"Good evening, Richard, I hope you don't mind me turning up unannounced. I've been told that you're going to be hosting some séance evenings." Frank said, as he stood in the doorway of number 106.

Frank was a tall, lean man and on this evening was wearing a grey smock, with a white shirt tucked in, emphasising the slimness of his waist. He combed his midnight black hair over his head which possibly covered a small bald spot. None the less, Frank looked extremely well presented and Richard felt comfortable inviting him in. Before Richard had time to question this man's intentions, he'd made his way through the hallway and taken a seat at the dinner table in the kitchen. Luckily his family were all upstairs. Frank continued;

"I don't have much experience with contacting the dead but I have an interest. I believe in life after death and that everyone's soul continues on somewhere; I'm looking for evidence that this is the case. God has created so much that I don't think he would have ended it with death. I can imagine you have had a great deal of interest in your séances but I do hope you might consider me, and let me get involved."

Richard was secretly thrilled at this man's interest in his spiritual meetings.

"The more the merrier, Frank, in fact I'm pleased you came tonight as I was keen to have an even number of people sitting. We have ten now, including you, which I think is a nice round figure. I will tell you, like I have informed the others, I don't claim to be a medium, spiritual healer or anything like that, I am just a curious man and as I have had a few experiences during my life, some of which quite recently, I am keen to find out what these ghosts or spirits, or whatever it is you want to call them, want from me and my family," Richard explained. "Do you have your own experiences?" he asked.

"Not really, just my beliefs and, although I'm religious, I have a pretty open mind." Frank replied.

Great, Richard thought. He was hoping he would have back up should anything happen or go wrong but he guessed he was pretty much on his own and now, not only were his family relying on him but he had other people depending on him too.

"I've asked people to be over tomorrow evening by eight o'clock, I hope that suits you," Richard said as more of a statement than a question, as even if Frank couldn't make the time he wasn't prepared to change it.

"Perfect. I'll see you then, and thanks again for letting me take part," Frank replied as he stood and walked over to the door. "By the way," he added, "apologise to your son if I woke him. He looked exhausted."

"What do you mean?" Richard asked, knowing that his children were all asleep in their beds. "What makes you think that you've woken them?   You've not even met them."

"Well, I presume he was your son. A small red headed boy was sitting in the armchair that's in the corner of the kitchen. He wouldn't take his eyes off of you. Didn't you see him?" Frank questioned rhetorically. "Anyway, my apologies again, I'll be off."

With that, Frank jumped down the porch and walked out of sight, leaving Richard standing frozen in the front porch. None of his children were awake and not one of them had red hair. Harry he thought, as he closed the door and turned around to look down the long, dark hallway into the kitchen. Although the light was on at the back of the house, it was hard to see anything further than the hall. He took a few steps forward as his mind raced through questions. Was he about to see the spirit of his childhood friend or was it just one of his own children asleep in the armchair waiting to be carried to bed? He knew which one he would have preferred.

As he walked closer to the kitchen he could smell a very sweet aroma; one which reminded him of the liquorice he used to buy from the old sweets shop nearby on his way home from school. In fact, the nostalgic smell brought back memories of his childhood friend who also favoured the sweet stuff. As he inhaled the sickly scent, he could hear a rustle coming from within the kitchen and, as he stepped inside and took hold of the door handle, he felt a cold breath on his face which smelt even sweeter than what filled the air around him. He was distracted for a second by the surreal sensation but, when he recovered, he was able to see the armchair in its pride of place, on the opposite side of the kitchen and, although there was no child lying in it, there was a piece of paper. Richard let go of the door handle which was keeping him stable and walked over to the chair. As he was close enough to see, he realised that it was in fact a photograph. The photograph from the cemetery he had taken all those years ago which had caught fire the night of his first Ouija board with Ellen but, now, it was intact in front of him and, more clearly than ever, Harry was standing behind the gravestone.

Tomorrow night can't come soon enough, he told himself, as he tore up the photograph and threw the remains in the bin.

*****

It was almost eight o'clock and the group began to arrive at his house. Although Richard's preference was for his family to be out of the house, it wasn't practical, so his wife and parents agreed to look after the children downstairs whilst he took his guests into the front room upstairs. He didn't want any of them to be involved, especially not his children, but it seemed that he had little choice. Everyone who he expected to turn up, did, as well as an older couple, Phyllis and Mike Shrober, who had heard about the gathering and thought that they would go along and join in.

"I hope you don't mind?" Phyllis asked. "Only we are both strong believers and I've always had a bit of a spiritual intuition so I think that you will benefit from my presence."

Phyllis was an elderly lady and Richard was partially concerned that she would suffer heart failure if anything like the occurrences of the last time should happen again.

"Yes, of course, that's fine," Richard replied, "Please make your way upstairs with the others, we are only waiting for a few more arrivals before we can start."

It was just one man Richard was waiting for, a man that had captured his interest; Frank Brately. Richard was anticipating his arrival as, of all those attending, Frank had the deepest beliefs and might have been able to offer some advice should anything untoward happen. Sure enough, just after eight, Frank showed up.

"Sorry about the delay, I got held up on my journey here. You know how it is. Now, where're we doing this thing?" he asked.

Richard laughed, "OK, no problem. Just make your way up the stairs, make a right when you get to the top and join everyone else. I'll be up in a minute."

Frank did as he was asked and left Richard downstairs, who made his way to the kitchen. He'd done a lot of reading into how to conduct a séance. He'd opted for a séance over a Ouija board as he was concerned about people not taking it seriously and moving the planchette themselves. He felt safer doing a séance to see how people responded and whether or not anything would come of it. He'd read that it was possible to involve stationary objects and encourage spirits to use

132

them by way of communication. Considering this, he decided that he would take into the séance a camera and a radio, both of which would have either a visual or aural impact that everyone would be able to witness. The radio was pretty self-explanatory and the camera was an old Polaroid type that Richard had used in his early career, so he was used to its mechanics. He deemed it imperative that everyone was able to witness any paranormal activity that may occur. He lifted both pieces of equipment from the kitchen worktop, and made his way upstairs to join the others.

In the front room, everyone was muttering amongst themselves and by the time Richard joined them they'd all become acquainted. Richard wasted no time with introductions and instead went straight into the proceedings that everyone was there for.

"Thanks for coming, everyone. As you all know, the purpose of this evening is to see if we are able to connect the spirit world. Yes, I'm referring to ghosts; souls of people who have moved from our world but cannot cross over to the next. Now, I believe that some spirits are confused about their deaths and try hard not to accept that they're dead. These spirits, along with other, evil ghosts who also refuse to pass over, are all stuck in limbo; a place that is somewhere between the living and the dead and exists parallel with the living and, sometimes, the living and the dead collide which is when we experience something that is paranormal. A Ouija board or séance can allow the two worlds to collide. I want to try to help those souls that need help, that are trapped and can't rest in peace. I have asked you here this evening to help me. As some of you may or may not know, I have had some experiences of my own which have brought me here and I'm hoping that the forthcoming evenings will enable me to answer questions that I've had since I was a child and I thank you all for allowing me to have this ability." Richard paused. "Anyway, this evening we will be conducting a séance. I am no expert but, to the best of my knowledge, this is when we will try to contact the dead by forming a circle with our hands, and building energy from within it to connect with those spirits around us. I cannot guarantee that it will work but I do have high hopes. I will first be placing a camera in the middle of the table. If we manage to contact something, we will ask it to use the camera in some way to communicate with us," he explained as he placed the camera in the middle of the large, round table he had moved into the room specifically for the evening. "If we can now all hold hands, alternating palms, so face your left palm up and your right palm down. There are a few rules."

"I'm not good with following rules," Frank mocked.

Richard looked at Frank, amused.

"As I'm the host, you must follow my lead. If I ask you to speak, then you must speak. If I tell you to move, then move. Please don't talk amongst yourselves, this can be quite distracting. The séance shouldn't last more than an hour but I am not timing it, so it could run longer. Under absolutely no circumstances should you break the chain. The chain that we will be forming using our hands is what will keep the entity at bay. It is the only thing that will stop anything we contact from following you home tonight. So hold tight, and only let go when the meeting is over and I give you the go ahead. Understood?" Richard questioned.

"Understood," everyone agreed in unison.

"Then let me begin." Richard blew out all but one candle beside him. "Please all now hold hands and repeat after me; if anyone is there, please give me a sign. If anyone's there, give us a sign. If anyone's there, give us a sign."

Everyone in the room began to chant with Richard. All those involved had high hopes for the evening. Some were keen to find out more about the afterlife, some eager to contact loved ones who had passed suddenly or died slowly. Everyone who sat around the large, solid oak table in 106 Poultney Road had a reason to be there but not one of them expected to be a part of something so real; so devastating that it would have such an impact on so many lives.

"What was that?" Phyllis asked from Richard's right hand side. "I'm sure I heard something..." She trailed off just as Jerry continued;

"It was footsteps; coming from the hallway. Richard, it's him. He's here again," Jerry said, panicking.

"Calm down, I didn't hear anything and, when we do, remind yourself that this is why we're all here. Now, please, can we continue? If anyone's there give me a sign."

Richard had been asking the question for almost twenty minutes and so far, besides a few anxious patrons, nothing had happened; until the candle blew out in a still air.

"I heard that," came a small voice.

"Me too," confirmed another. "Richard?"

Richard sat there, in the pitch black, holding onto every sound; the ticking clock, a beating heart, a racing breath; footsteps.

"OK, we have someone here with us. I can hear you walking down the hallway behind me. Are you in the room with us? If you are, please give us a sign. Use the camera on the table, or make some kind of noise within the room. We are here to help you," Richard said with such certainty that he almost lost his breath speaking the words.

The room fell silent. No one spoke and there wasn't a sound to be heard. The silence was so intense that it was difficult for any of them to concentrate on anything besides their own heartbeat. Everyone was sitting completely still, in the hope that they may encounter something unexplainable. Richard let his eyes roam the room, trying to see someone or something he could focus on. He could make outlines of the unfamiliar people that sat around him, in his home that he had opened up to them, in the hope that they could help him put his past to rest.

As if from nowhere, there was a distant sound of music; a very soft, hymn-like melody filled the room around them. Everyone froze apart from Paul, who tried to stand, but Margaret pulled him back down in his seat.

"Don't break the chain," she urged whilst restraining him.

No one else dared move as the melody continued to play. Richard, without having to assess the situation, knew that the music was coming from beneath the table, where he'd placed the radio earlier, with the intention of placing it in the centre of the table once they'd finished with the camera, which was still in front of him on the table.

"No one panic," he told those around him in the darkened room. "It would seem we've someone here with us. Thank you for making your presence known. You've made the radio beneath us play music, now I would like for you to work the camera on the table. If you're still with us, take a photograph. Speak with me, everyone," he urged. "If there's anyone there, take a photograph. If there's anyone there, take a photograph," he asked repeatedly, with his group members chanting the words with him. As the group grew louder, so did the music and it became a battle between the two. As the volume increased, so did the energy and the determination from those within the room until, from nowhere, there was the brightest flash from the camera sitting in the middle of the table, and a small, square photograph slid from within it.

"It worked," Richard whispered to himself in disbelief.

"Unbelievable," said Margaret.

Desperate to see what was on the film, Richard ended the séance as quickly as he knew how. He recited the Lord's Prayer, and cajoled everyone to repeat the prayer with him afterwards. He then asked for all spirits to leave and not out-stay their welcome and, with that, he broke the chain and grabbed the photo, running downstairs to his bedroom, to develop it.

"I'll be right back," he told his guests as he left them in the room.

He burst through the door and pinned the photo to the line he had hanging from each wall.

"Are you alright?" Ellen asked as he bashfully entered the bedroom.

Within minutes he could see the print coming through on the glossy paper. The first thing he noticed was that the photograph was of the room in which the séance took place. It was missing all furnishings and decoration; no paper hung on the walls, or light fixtures around the bulbs; just a large, empty space, concealing nothing. He took hold of the photo and looked at it for a minute or two, trying to grasp its significance but he came to no conclusion.

"Sorry, sweetheart," Richard continued to face the wall with his back to his wife. "You won't believe what's happened. It's best I check this thoroughly and explain later," he said, glancing over at Ellen who was now sitting up in their bed, as he made his way back out of the bedroom and upstairs, to re-join the group.

One by one, they all studied the photograph and speculated about how and why the photo had been taken. As it was a Polaroid, it was only possible for it to take a photograph of its mirror reflection in front of the lens, and yet not a single person that had witnessed it being taken appeared in the photo.

A couple of hours after they had arrived, Richard's guests began to leave. Frank was the last to go. Surprisingly, he'd been quiet all evening. Richard thought that even he'd been shocked by what he'd witnessed; no one had expected the evening to turn out the way it did and were all already discussing the next meeting. Ellen had her head deep in a book long after she'd put the children to bed and his parents had made their way upstairs to their bedrooms when the guests began to leave. As he closed the door behind Frank, he laid up against it, looking down the long hallway into his house. A house that has seen it all, he thought.

He gathered his thoughts and turned out the light as he made his way to the bathroom to get himself ready for bed. As he made his way down the hall, he passed the foot of the staircase and, as he did, a flash of light filled the hallway upstairs. He stood momentarily; still nervous from the events that had taken place earlier that evening, he froze. Thud-thud-thud. Footsteps running across the room above his head, the room where the séance had taken place; he had left the camera on the table and the flash must have just gone off again.

He called quietly up the stairs, thinking that someone, perhaps one of his children, was awake and messing about.

"Hello?" he called but there was no answer.

He knew his family were all asleep in their beds. He knew that he was the only one awake.

Without realising, he'd already made his way halfway up the dingy staircase with his back against the bitterly cold wall behind him and the opening of the staircase above. As he reached the top, he found himself rushing towards the room, eager to see if he was right and another photograph had been taken. As he fell in through the door and switched on the light, there in front of him lay a white sheet of glossy paper. I was bloody right, he thought. He turned the light off as fast as he could so that it wouldn't spoil the development and quickly made his way back down the stairs, trying not to think too much about where the photo had come from. He rushed into the kitchen, opened up the drawer to find a match. He lit a candle and placed it down next to him on the table and opened his hand out in front of him to reveal the photo. At first he just stared at it, trying to figure out what was in front of him. Whilst he knew the surroundings, they were hard to place. It was the chair that he recognised initially. It was the chair behind him that sat in the corner of the kitchen. The photograph was in the kitchen. How is that possible? he asked himself, but what really disgusted him, what made him sick to the stomach, was the main focal point of the picture. Sitting on the chair, that he had turned to see, empty behind him, was Ellen, naked. She was leaning back with her body tightened and rigid, her face frozen, expressionless and whilst Richard couldn't take his eyes off her face, he was utterly distracted by the hundreds of tiny, naked babies that were clinging to her body. She was covered from head to foot with miniature, perfectly formed, babies that appeared to be sucking on her skin, their mouths clinging to her body.

Although completely revolted, Richard couldn't help but be fascinated by the impossible photograph he had before him. As he sat there, in silence, looking at the demonic image of his wife, he swallowed down the terrifying realisation that if someone had taken this picture after the séance, after his guests had left and his family were asleep in bed, that he was not the only one who was awake, looking at the photograph. Someone, or something, was there with him, admiring their handy-work.

142

Chapter Twelve

His first séance was the talk of the pub, so it was hard to keep anything from his family. Richard hadn't wanted to tell anyone about the two photographs; he didn't want to encourage panic or anymore curiosity than what there already was. A week had passed and nothing untoward had happened since his meeting, so Richard was trying to believe that he had somehow managed to put whatever it was that was haunting the house to rest but, deep down, he knew the truth and, in fact, he was getting more and more interested in the supernatural.

All of the attendees of the first séance were keen to be involved again and asked when the next one would be. Richard had decided that he didn't want any more spectators and would stick with the original ten people for the next sitting. He'd decided to wait a few weeks and scheduled the second séance for October 2nd.

Of all his family, Ellen had been the most inquisitive. She'd asked question after question about his first séance and Richard had been forthcoming about most of what had happened; he didn't like hiding things from his wife but he also didn't find it necessary to tell her about the horrid photograph that had appeared after everyone had left. He didn't want her any more scared than she already was but Ellen seemed to be more intrigued by the events rather than scared. Up until now, she had been happy with hearing the stories and of Richard's experiences, but now she wanted to get involved.

"I'd like to sit with you this evening, Richard, when you're doing your séance. I'd like to see how it's done. Please, would you let me?" Ellen asked.

"I'm not sure, Ellen, I don't like the idea of you involving yourself, anyway it's good that you keep the kids occupied and out of the way," Richard replied.

"Don't use the boys as an excuse, Richard, your parents are more than capable to look after them," she reminded him. "Come on, just this once, just so that I'm not left in the dark. I like to know what's going on in my own house."

It wasn't that Richard didn't trust his wife or that he was worried about her behaviour or anything of the sort; he was terrified that last time, whatever it was that he had contacted, had involved her. The thought had filled his nightmares ever since. How could he let her attend a séance when it seemed that she was the main focus of them already? However, on the other hand, he didn't feel that he had the authority over his wife to dictate to her. He wasn't one of those men who bossed his wife around, he respected her and her decisions and therefore decided to be honest with her and tell her what had happened and let her make her own mind up. He explained that more had happened the last time than he'd originally told her, and went to fetch the evidence. When presented with the photograph of her naked

144

body covered with those tiny creatures which resembled human babies, she was grateful for her husband's original story.

"Now you see why I kept this from you and why I'm not keen on you being with us when we do the séance this evening? It's because I think that whatever it is, that keeps contacting me, is drawn in by my life and those who are in it. I don't want you to be in anymore danger than we may already be in," Richard explained.

"You think we're in danger?" Ellen asked, concerned not only for her safety, but also for their family.

"No, not as such but I do feel intimidated and I want to find out more about the photos and the music and the presence that I've been feeling for years. You understand that, right?" he asked, tenderly kissing Ellen's forehead. "It's your job to make sure the kids are OK."

Ellen smiled up at her husband and nodded in agreement. After seeing that picture, she no longer wanted to be involved.

*****

The same as before, people began to arrive at Poultney Road from eight that evening and not long after, everyone had made their way upstairs to the same front bedroom as before. This time, Richard had left in the original furniture, which included a small brown fabric sofa and a wooden dresser that had its place in the corner of the room, hiding where the man in black was last seen. Although he'd originally chosen to keep the photograph of Ellen a secret, he had since decided that everyone had the right to know what they were getting involved in; the fact that Ellen had been targeted and she hadn't attended the séance meant that they could contact anyone or anything on the other side, regardless of its intentions or interest. He handed round the first photograph of the empty room in which they all stood and, as everyone inspected the first, Richard explained;

"Now some of you may find the next photo a little disturbing. I know that even I feel a little uncomfortable looking at it, but you must understand the power these séances can have and the energy that they conjure. It would seem that even those not present can be involved in a connection."

He passed the photo to Frank, who was sitting directly to his left. Frank sat for a moment, speechless, looking at the image he held in front of him.

"Impossible," he said, as he eyed the photo carefully. "Have you shown Ellen?" he asked as he passed the photograph onto Mike, who reacted similarly.

"I have and, in fact, it's the reason she hasn't joined us tonight. It could be possible that something connected with us the last time to try to contact her, and sending an image like this could mean all manner of things but neither one of us want her involved further."

"I don't blame you," Frank said, a shiver passing down his spine as he recalled the image of the man in black that they'd seen during the last séance.

"OK, so now that you all know the true purpose of these meetings, I would like to proceed," Richard suggested to the rest of the group. "As before, I'd like us all to hold hands and again, remember the rules of my séances. This time I'm not going to be using any props and instead will be encouraging the spirits to communicate through objects that are in the room. I will allow them to use me, if necessary, and use all of us to build energy. If there is anyone here who is not comfortable with this, then I suggest you make me aware now and perhaps leave the meeting and come again next month."

Everyone sat, sharing eye contact with one another in silence.

"OK, I take it that everyone is happy to continue. As before, repeat after me; if anyone is there, give us a sign. If anyone is there, give us a sign." Richard chanted this for at least five minutes, whilst everyone else joined in.

A further eight or nine minutes passed when Stephen started to move uncomfortably in his chair.

"Everything OK, Stephen?" Jack asked, as he could feel Stephen's awkward grip.

"I don't know," he answered sharply. "I'm very hot; is it hot in here?" he asked as the sweat trickled its way down from his forehead to his chin.

"Perhaps we should stop, Richard?" Jack requested. "He doesn't look so good."

Everyone dropped the chants, but Richard wasn't keen to stop the séance.

"Stephen, the choice is ultimately yours. I think you're reacting like this either because you're uncomfortable with this situation or someone is trying to contact you," said Richard, trying to reassure Stephen whose breathing was speeding up rapidly. "Either way, it could be worth continuing; if we back down now we may lose a connection."

Richard knew he was being selfish. He could see that Stephen was clearly distressed, but wasn't prepared to lose touch with a spirit should they have contact. He had no real reason to be concerned for Stephen's welfare as surely, he was just nervous. Richard didn't know Stephen as a friend, purely as an acquaintance who'd been put in touch with him through a friend of a friend, so he had nothing to lose. Richard started to continue but was stopped abruptly.

"Something's wrong, something's very wrong. Oh dear God, it hurts so much. My back!" he said as he stood from the table, arching his back. "I'm going to have to break the chain. I can't bear the pain. Richard, say a prayer. Say it quick, I can't hold on much longer," he yelled out in distress.

Richard uttered the Lord's Prayer as quickly as he knew how and, as soon as he'd finished, Stephen threw his arms to the buttons of his shirt and started tearing his way through them.

"Help me someone, please!" Stephen begged. "There's something wrong with my back."

Whilst Jack and Frank were pulling at the buttons, everyone, except Richard, stood in anticipation as the men worked to get his top off as fast as they could. As Richard made his way around the table, he stopped in his tracks he caught sight of the back of Stephen's shirt. It was a cream-and-brown striped pattern which looked clean of any marks or stains from the front. In the upper centre of his back, blood had soaked all the way through the shirt, about three inches across by two inches down. The blood looked dark and thick, the freshest kind, and as the men removed the shirt, Richard gasped at what he saw. What they were witnessing was impossible. Richard's brain worked frantically trying to piece together possibilities but to no avail. There was no explanation.

"What is it? Tell me, please I'm in agony," Stephen pleaded as he twisted and turned his torso in a desperate attempt to see what was causing his pain.

Richard and the other two men stared in disbelief at Stephen's bloodied body and at the minuscule writing that was being inscribed on his bare skin. It was as if an invisible, sharp instrument was burning or slicing through the outer layers of his flesh, gashing it open and making it ooze the thick, red liquid that had already drenched his shirt.

"Arrggghhh!" Stephen cried out. "Someone tell me what's happening."

"I don't know how to explain this best but it would seem that you have some kind of message burnt into your skin," Richard explained. "Jack, go get me some cotton wool from the bathroom cupboard at the end of the hall and cover it in warm water," he requested as Jack was already through the bedroom door and running down the landing.

When he returned, he handed it to Richard, who tried his best to soak up the excess blood.

"Ouch!" Stephen cried.

"Sorry, but I need to clear the blood to be able to see what it is."

Everyone else stood still, completely motionless; unable to believe what was unfolding in front of them.

"OK, I think I can make sense of this," Richard said, handing the blood stained cotton wool back to Jack, who was standing next to him.

"I'm so sorry Stephen, I love you & I'll always be with you. Janice. Stephen, does this mean anything to you? Who's Janice?" Richard probed.

"Oh dear God, no; it can't be. I have to go. I have to make sure she's OK," Stephen rambled whilst grabbing his shirt and making his way to the door.

"But who's Janice?" asked Juliette who'd been sitting eagerly, waiting for the facts to unfold.

"She's my fiancé. We found out this morning that she's pregnant," Stephen said, in a daze. "I have to go, I hope you understand."

And with that he dashed through the hall, down the stairs and out the front door, slamming it closed behind him and leaving everyone stunned, sitting around the table, unable to process what had happened.

*****

It was later that week that Richard and the others found out the truth behind what happened to Stephen and his fiancé that evening, as word soon spread among the regulars of the Old Bell.

Stephen was a hard grafter and would often help his dad on site wherever he was working as a builder. He had seen Janice one day walking home from school, she was only sixteen but her long blonde hair and curvaceous figure left

151

men twice her age drooling after her well-proportioned derriere. He'd a rough idea of her age and, as he looked far younger than his twenty-five years, decided to follow her home one day and build up enough courage to speak to her. Janice was taken aback by Stephen's cool introduction and was happy to arrange to see him on her way home from school the following day and the next, and so it continued for almost a month. It was only then that Stephen suggested their going to the cinema and seeing a black-and-white comedy, Just William's Luck. He thought it would give him the opportunity to get to know Janice better.

"I think it's probably best that I meet you at the pictures. Although my parents aren't strict, they mightn't be too proud of me spending time with an older man. For now they can think I'm spending time with my girlfriends from school."

Although a little hurt by her suggestion, Stephen understood and met Janice at the cinema at six that Saturday evening. Inside, he had attempted the yawn-stretch-arm-around shoulder-move and it worked on Janice a treat. He guessed that it was the first time she'd been so close to someone of the opposite sex and was aroused by the challenge. The secret affair was extremely exciting for Stephen and when he was walking Janice home after sharing a drink together in Kathryn's Café, Stephen lead Janice down a side street which lead them to the rear of her parents' house. Out of sight of passers-by, he moved towards his young quarry and kissed her rose-stained lips gently, leaving her eager for more. She reciprocated his request and, before long, they shared a passionate embrace. Although experienced with women, Stephen had never been quite so enflamed by such an inexperienced lover. Her naïveté and innocence destroyed his ability to hold back, and he lost control of his actions. Meanwhile Janice, fuelled by passion and encouraging the moment, gently tugged at Stephen's zip-fly. He felt the gentle caress of his virginal beauty's touch and before long had done the inevitable; slept with a girl almost half his age and stolen her virtue, her purity, and had ultimately left her feeling ashamed.

He returned the next day to the place they had been meeting daily for the past month but there was no sign of Janice. He even visited her school to try to catch her on her way out but it was as though she'd disappeared. Two months passed and Stephen didn't hear a word from her until, one day, Janice turned up at the site where he was working.

"Where've you been?" Stephen demanded. "I've been worried sick. I've really missed you," he added.

"I'm sorry, you're not the only one who was worried, my parents almost had a fit when I came home last week. I've been staying with my aunt and uncle in Portsmouth. I needed to get away and find time to think. I'm sorry."

"No need to explain," Stephen replied, "you're home now and that's all that matters."

"I'm sorry to tell you that I come with news. I'm unsure whether it'll be good or bad news in your opinion but, unfortunately, it's news I must share," she said, looking down at her feet whilst pushing gravel with the points of her black lace-up shoes. "I'm pregnant."

Both of them stood silent. Janice avoided all eye contact whilst Stephen searched his mind for something to say. What could he say? He wasn't ready to be a father, he had his whole life ahead of him.

"I don't know what to say to you. What do you want me to say? I'm not ready for this, Janice, I don't want to be a dad," he said, not able to look her in the eye. "You understand that, don't you?"

"Regardless of whether or not you want to be a dad, you're going to be one. I'm not getting rid of this child, I just can't do it. My parents are going to be devastated that their daughter is pregnant at sixteen and hasn't got the support of the father. They would have been right about you without even meeting you. Thanks for nothing!" she shouted as tears flooded her cheeks. She turned on her heel, not waiting for his reply.

Stephen left work early that day and took the long route home. He thought about his life, his aspirations and what he wanted to achieve. The more he thought, the more he realised that he did in fact want children and settle down one day and, although the timing wasn't ideal, he'd do the honourable thing and ask the mother of his child to be his wife.

He knew where Janice lived, so the next day made his way to her house and when he realised no one was home, he decided to wait for her on the porch. Almost an hour passed before he caught sight of her walking around the corner. She wasn't alone, she was accompanied by an older woman, who could have been her twin sister had there not been an obvious age gap. Great, the mother-in-law, he thought.

"Stephen, what are you doing here?" Janice asked as she and her mother approached. "Mother, this is my friend, Stephen. Stephen, my mother."

"It's a pleasure to meet you, Mrs Nash, but please may I have a few words with your daughter in private?" he requested.

"Well, so long as that's alright with you, Janice?" she responded, waiting for her daughter's nod, and then made her way inside, leaving them outside alone.

"What do you have to say now, Stephen?" Janice asked. "I have to tell my parents this evening that I'm pregnant, I can't leave it any longer because I'll start showing," she explained, speaking quietly, not wanting her mother to overhear. "I'm scared, Stephen."

"Well, it's a good job that I'm here to support you then, isn't it," Stephen said with a grin on his face. "I barely know you and I sure as hell don't know this one yet," he said, gesturing towards her stomach, "but I want to and I want to know you better, Janice," he said as he lowered himself onto

155

one knee. "I haven't got any money to offer you, a roof to put over your head or even a ring to put on your finger, but I will, and for now I have my life and love. I was wrong before, I am ready to be a dad and if I'm ever going to be ready to be a husband, now is as good a time as any. So, Janice, will you marry me?"

Janice pulled Stephen to his feet and jumped into his arms.

"Thank you," she said, "it means a lot to me."

It was a glorious afternoon, so they took a stroll together. They talked for at least an hour about what and how they would tell people of the news and their relationship, and even began speaking of the baby and possible names. They decided to hold off telling Janice's parents for a day or two. Stephen had plans that evening that he wanted to keep and it also gave him enough time to build up some courage; he believed he needed it. He left Janice outside her parents' house and headed straight to number 106 Poultney Road, where he had a meeting to attend.

Janice never went back home that evening; she never even made it past the front gate. She had paper and a pen in her rucksack that she had across her back, and walked to the park a mile or so from her house. She sat herself on a cold, wooden bench and began to write her letter addressed to Stephen. She didn't want to ruin his life and she didn't want to bring shame to her family; she couldn't bear telling her parents and seeing their disappointment. Stephen wasn't the one who wasn't ready to settle down and become a parent; it was Janice.

Chapter Thirteen

The story of Stephen Pillar soon circulated and everyone was getting in touch with Richard, either over a beer at the Old Bell or turning up at his house unexpectedly. Richard didn't want anyone to get hurt or be frightened by what he was doing. What had happened that night had frightened him, so he could only imagine how scared Stephen must have been. To then discover that his fiancé and mother of his unborn child had committed suicide, was just hideous. Richard decided not to have any more public meetings and to instead concentrate on his career and making money for his family. He told Ellen of the events so that she didn't hear it from someone else, but he managed to be as vague as possible when explaining to his parents, though it was their house too and they had a right to know the truth about what was happening. Everyone seemed to be in the same frame of mind as Richard, and agreed to stop all séances, Ouija boards and any other form of spiritual contact. Even though they made no effort to form new connections, the connections they'd already made wanted to hang around.

The boys grew up blissfully unaware of the house and its visitors and lived perfectly normal childhoods. Keith, from a young age, appeared to be the most receptive of the three. He shared the first bedroom downstairs with his older brother, Eric. It was a deceptively spacious room and now that the boys had turned four and six, they had two small-sized beds in there as well as a wardrobe, chest-of-drawers and desk. Although it was a big room, they didn't spend too much time in there, they both enjoyed being outside and playing family board games with their older brother and parents. None of the boys had been bothered by any paranormal activity for a while and were all too young to remember what had happened years ago. Of an evening, Keith and Eric would go to bed a little earlier than Robert; it was either Flo or Henry who would read them a bedtime story, turn out the light and close the bedroom door behind them, leaving the boys to sleep through until morning. It was January 11th, 1947 when it was first bought to Flo's attention that something wasn't right with Keith. He had his bath in the family bathroom upstairs but instead of his usual request to get out before he was finished, he took his time, playing with water, his floatation toys and kicking up a bit of a fuss when either Richard or Ellen tried to get him out.

"Come on Keith, it's time to get out, sweetheart, or you'll shrivel up like a prune. Check your fingers, I bet they're all wrinkled," Ellen asked of him.

Keith looked down at his fingertips and just as his mum had told him, they were all wrinkled up like an old man's face. Keith giggled.

He stood up and raised his arms in the air for his mother to lift him out.

"I don't have to go straight to bed do I, Mummy?" he asked. "Can you read me a long story?"

"We'll have to see about that, you'll have to be extra nice to Nanny and Granddad," Ellen replied, hoping this would make him behave a little before bedtime.

As usual, Keith brushed his teeth alongside his brother, Eric, ran downstairs to kiss his big brother, Robert, and dad goodnight and made his way to be with Eric. He climbed into bed and pulled the eiderdown up under his chin.

"Please can you read me a story, I'm not tired yet, Nanny." He told Flo.

"Of course I can, Keith, I always do," She answered, opening his thick book of bedtime stories.

As she began to read, so Keith and Eric listened intently until their eyelids became heavy and began to close; it was the soothing sound of Flo's voice that sent them both into a deep and dream welcoming sleep.

*****

At least three or four hours passed when Keith was woken suddenly. He sat up as he heard a sharp knocking sound coming from the right-hand corner of the room. His brother, Eric, slept peacefully in his bed opposite his brother, and although the sound of Eric's deep breathing usually comforted his younger brother, tonight there was nothing that would ease his nerves.

It was the same as the night before when he'd been woken in the early hours, but by what he didn't know. The previous night, he'd investigated the sound of footsteps that were running up and down the hallway outside his bedroom but, when he opened the door, there was no one there. He'd thought that maybe Robert was doing it to frighten him but when he didn't tease him at breakfast, he knew that wasn't the case. Tonight it was different; the sounds were coming from within the bedroom and the door was closed. He sat for a moment in the silence, waiting to hear the noise again and, when it never came, he hid beneath his deep blue bed sheets in hope that he wouldn't be frightened again. As he lay there, he listened to Eric's breathing, a continuous hum that was so hypnotic, he felt himself drifting back to sleep. He was relaxing once again, the warmth around him and the feeling of not being alone almost sent him back to sleep, but his peace was broken yet again by the sound of the door handle of the bedroom being pushed down and the catch clicking open. Still with his head beneath the covers, he didn't dare move; for a moment, he was paralysed by fear. Unable to scream, he just lay there and waited. Once again he listened to the sound of heavy breathing coming from where his brother slept. Nothing else in the room moved; no sounds or unfamiliar noises, just the continual inhaling and exhaling coming from his sleeping sibling. As he focused on his brother, the breathing that had continued for the past five minutes was suddenly accompanied by a second breath, one that sounded much deeper, slower than Eric's and it appeared to be coming from the other side of the room, towards the door. Keith clenched the covers that he had pulled above his head and, as his little hands trembled along with the rest of his body, slowly pulled the cover so that he was able to peer from underneath. He opened his eyes but was hit by the heavy darkness that surrounded him. The dark brown curtains shielded any light from entering the bedroom; he blinked ferociously to adjust to the pitch black. As he did, he could see the white outline of the bedroom door. It wasn't closed like his mother had left it; it was instead, open about six inches. He pushed himself upright, still clenching the edge of his eiderdown as he clenched and wiggled his buttocks to slowly move closer to the end of his bed so that he could see better. As he dragged himself along, he didn't once lose sight of the opened door and, as he drew himself closer, he was able to see that there was something on the other side of the door, looking in. He closed his eyes and counted to three but when he opened them again, instead of the image disappearing, he was able to see the man standing there more clearly.

Although Keith wasn't able to see the man fully, with half of his body hidden behind the door, he was able to see that the man was of average height, with a stocky physique, and was wearing a long black raincoat with a tall top hat. Although the small child didn't recognise the man, he cracked a smile at Keith and slowly pushed the door further open. Fear swallowed Keith up from his insides and made it impossible for him to move, or to scream, he just froze in his unprotected position, sheltered only by the comfort of the

163

quilt which he had yanked up to his chin. The man took each heavy step slowly, and quite purposefully, towards the end of Keith's bed, not once taking his eyes off the young boy. Keith was desperate for Eric to wake up, to witness what was happening, to see this man that had been visiting him each night. As the man came closer, Keith tried to study his face but it was too dark, too well hidden by the shadow of his hat. It was when the man reached the end of Keith's bed, and was no more than three feet from him, that Keith let go of the eiderdown, threw his hands over his eyes and let out a high pitched scream that woke the entire house. The scream was utterly terrifying and Eric almost fell from his mattress in terror. Within seconds, Richard and Ellen came bursting into the room and switched on the light. Ellen ran straight to Keith's bedside.

"Baby, what's wrong? What's happened? Did you have a bad dream?" she asked, trying to pull his hands away from his eyes. "Sweetheart, it's OK. Mummy and Daddy are here with you, everything's fine."

With his eyes closed, Keith threw his arms around his mum's neck and began to sob.

"Mummy, there's a man in here. A scary looking man. He was trying to get me," he explained and as he did Eric, who was making his way back under his eiderdown, similarly voiced his fear and incomprehension.

"What does he mean, Mummy? What man?" Eric asked as he turned to look at Richard.

Ellen too, turned to face her husband, at a loss for any words of comfort. Both parents sat, staring, thinking, without saying a word but trying to rationalise what was going on and to look unconcerned in front of their children.

"It was only Uncle, darling. He came to see me and your daddy but, because we were asleep, he came to check on both of you. Don't be scared of him," Ellen said, trying to comfort her terrified children. "He left as soon as he upset you, he didn't mean to scare you so don't be frightened but you must tell me or Daddy if he ever comes again. OK?" Ellen asked.

"OK," Keith answered, "so why did he come back tonight when he has already been here last night?" Keith asked innocently.

"This isn't the first time he's been here?" Richard asked.

"I don't think so, I heard someone here last night too. They kept running up and down the hallway which kept me awake. Was that Uncle too?" Keith asked inquisitively.

"I think it must have been, yes." Richard replied. "Did you hear this too, Eric?" he asked.

"No I didn't, Daddy," he replied. "Can we go back to sleep now, I'm tired," he said as he turned to face the wall.

Richard and Ellen kissed both their children goodnight, turned out the light, but this time left the door open. They made their way back to bed without saying a word, climbed into bed and lay in silence.

"I don't want you ever touching another Ouija board Richard, this has gone too far now," Ellen demanded, turning her back on her husband without waiting for or wanting a reply.

*****

A month or so passed and neither Eric nor Keith mentioned seeing any more men or unwanted people in the house. It was obvious to Ellen that this was the reason Keith acted so strangely that night at bedtime and, without any more odd behaviour, she presumed that everything was now OK. The Camps carried on their lives as usual; Robert, and now Eric too, spending their days at school, Flo and Henry looking after Keith and spending time with friends whilst Ellen spent the days looking for work and Richard continued to develop his photography business. Life was good, and number 106 was a happy place to be.

It was a Friday evening and Ellen had been lucky enough to get herself a job working in a bank during the day. She arranged with Flo that whilst she was able to drop the boys at school before spending the day at work, Flo would look after Keith and collect the kids from school. Ellen arrived home by four-thirty and cooked for all the family on two

166

nights a week whilst three nights she would cook for just Richard and the boys. It was handy having the two kitchens in the house and allowed the three generations to live their lives separately when they wanted to. This particular Friday, Ellen was cooking. The whole family enjoyed the meal and finished off the night with a game of Monopoly. As usual, no one won, they gave up before a winner was determined. The boys had their baths and went to bed. Flo and Henry made their way upstairs whilst Richard and Ellen cleaned up. Climbing into bed, Ellen was unusually tired, the new job and long days having taken their toll on her, and she fell into a deep sleep before she was able to evaluate the busy day she'd had.

*****

She had no idea what the time was or how long she'd been asleep, but Ellen woke whilst the sky was still dark. Although her eyes wouldn't adjust, she could sense that someone else was in the room, watching her. At first she thought it must be Richard, lying next to her; she thought that perhaps he'd woken up before her and couldn't sleep, but as well as his eyes being closed, his deep breathing was a tell-tale sign he was sound asleep. She looked at the door thinking that one of her children would be standing in the doorway, waiting for her to wake up to tell her they didn't feel well or couldn't sleep, but the door was empty. She laid herself back down and closed her eyes.

You're too tired to be awake, you're imagining things, she told herself.

She relaxed into her pillow and turned herself over ready to fall back into the unknown realm of dreams and nightmares but as she settled herself and tried to lift the eiderdown closer to her cheek, she felt that the quilt was restricted; like someone was holding it from the other end. Presuming it was Richard, she yanked on it but with no avail. She reached her arm behind her to feel for Richard and he was just where she knew he would be. To her discomfort, the cover was hanging loosely between the two of them which meant that Richard wasn't the one holding the quilt back; someone, or something else, must be. Ellen lay still without moving, holding her breath for fear of what she may see if she dared to look. She waited a moment or two before trying to pull on the cover once again but, the same as before, it wouldn't budge. Her knees were pulled up tightly to her chest, in the usual foetal position she slept in, but she decided to stretch her legs down so that she was able to feel whether anything was confining her movement on the bed. As she slowly stretched out her limbs under the soft feel of the cotton material that lay on top of her, not only keeping her warm but also shielding her from harm, they were prevented from stretching fully by something heavy on top of the covers.

Ellen sharply pulled her knees back into her; what on earth is happening? She asked herself whilst trying to gain yet more courage to look at what was accompanying her, and

168

her husband, in their bedroom. She squeezed her eyes tightly shut and counted slowly in her head; one, two, she paused for a moment, three. She sat bolt upright in her bed and turned to face whatever was with her in the bedroom and, as she did, she instantaneously wished she hadn't. Sitting on the bottom of the bed was a man. Although Ellen wasn't able to see fully because of the restricted light in the room, her eyes had adjusted somewhat and she was able to determine that the man was dressed entirely in black from head to foot. With his right side facing her, he was staring at the wall ahead. Although she tried, she was unable to make out the man's face, any features or details of what he looked like. She could however see that the skin on his face was pale in the moonlight that had made its way through a small gap in the curtains. She was unable to look at his hands or any other part of his body, as he was covered from head to toe in black clothing, gloves, hat and shoes. As Ellen became more acquainted with the image in front of her, the meaning of everything that Richard had ever said suddenly dawned on her; about why he was keen on doing the Ouija boards, and why he was scared to do more. It was because of the man in black. The man who had first visited him on his way to school the day his friend died; the man that he'd seen in their house; the man that he was terrified of. As Ellen was flooded with fear of the man, or entity, sitting before her, she was desperately reaching out for her husband, unable to find contact, to try to wake him. She realised that she was still holding her breath, unable to breathe and, whilst desperately reaching out to Richard who was still asleep next to her, the man in black slowly turned his face to look at her; to stare his deathly black eyes into hers and, as he grimaced, a smile baring a stale mouth full of dirty yellowed teeth, she found it deep within her to scream and throw herself onto her husband.

*****

Richard woke instantly, panicking and searching for the bedside light as his wife hid her face deep within his chest.

"He's here, Richard, please, please make him go away," she pleaded.

Richard rummaged the room with his eyes, looking for whomever his wife seemed so terrified of.

"Who is Ellen? Who's here?" Richard probed. "There's no one here besides me and you. Look," he said whilst lifting his wife's head from the crook of his neck. "You must have been dreaming, sweetheart, it's just us," he said reassuringly.

Ellen lifted her head and slowly turned to face where the man had been sitting.

"He was sitting just there, Richard. It was him, the man in black. He was here. I was so scared. Hold me, please," Ellen begged. "I've never been so afraid, Richard, why didn't you wake up? I needed you," she said as she began to cry.

Richard comforted his wife until she fell asleep in his arms, and until the sun rose. He had no idea whether what his wife had witnessed was real or whether it was part of a dream or nightmare. A small part of Richard told himself that it wasn't a dream and the man in black had been back in their house that night, in their room, watching them, waiting for them; waiting for his wife. The thought made him shudder but, as tiredness overcame him and the room offered light, and with it comfort, he finally fell back into an uncertain sleep.

I left the house on Poultney Road without saying another word to Mrs Robinson. She would have thought I was rude, a time waster; either way I wouldn't be seeing her again. I would never go back to that house. Elliott followed me out the front door whilst trying to grab a hold of me, to hold me whilst I tried to gain control but I couldn't speak, I could only move as fast as my legs would take me.

"What's wrong? What happened?" Elliott asked, slamming the car door shut as he climbed inside.

I wouldn't answer, I just leant back into the headrest of my seat and took in a deep, controlled breath. I wanted to tell Elliott, I really did, but he wouldn't believe me. I'm sure he would want to but he didn't see anything and he wouldn't be able to comprehend that I'd seen something that he wasn't able to. I questioned for a moment whether I believed that he wasn't able to see such things or whether, in fact, it was because he didn't want to see them that meant he couldn't.

"Nothing's wrong, I just freaked out," I said reassuringly, perhaps a little implausibly but Elliott didn't probe further. "Let's go home."

I turned the key in the ignition and drove away.

I had, at last, done it; I'd visited the house on Poultney Road that, throughout my upbringing, I'd heard so much

173

about. Was it what I had expected? No, it wasn't but perhaps it had been worse than I'd imagined it to be. I ask myself what I thought the house would be, or feel like, and I think in my head I would have made it more obviously haunted; the pain visible in the walls, a smell or stench which marked the presence of ghosts or spirits. But it's not as easy as that. This house, I know, is haunted from its deepest roots but yet it conceals it so well. I went into the house eagerly looking for evidence, signs that something did exist there and I was given that proof but still I knew that the next innocent family or couple to walk through the entrance would have no idea of what they were getting themselves into. It made me sick to the stomach, yet I knew that I wasn't in a position to change their fate.

When we got home, I let Elliott get on with dinner whilst I took myself upstairs and ran a bath. I would often relax this way after dinner but tonight the thought of food made me sick. I couldn't stop thinking about what I'd seen; her face. The innocence behind her eyes; my eyes. I couldn't get the image out of my head. What did it mean? How could I be trapped in the house when I'd never before set foot inside? It occurred to me that perhaps I'd been searching so hard for so long to find answers, and some kind of reason for what had happened inside number 106, that I'd somehow manifested myself into the hell that was standing on Poultney Road.

I shudder at the thought and feel myself prickle over the length of my body, hairs standing on end as I remember something my Uncle Robert had told me when I was first researching and questioning my family about the events that took place inside the house. I asked him whether he'd moved on from what happened to him and his family all those years ago and, although I think that he'd like to believe that he has, deep down, he knew the answer was no. He went on to describe a recurring dream that he'd had for about ten years.

*****

The setting was inside the house. He explained that in the dream, he would always be upstairs. He described his surroundings as familiar but dark and cold, the atmosphere stark. He could hear people talking and laughing downstairs, he presumed the people he could hear were his family. In the dream, he'd walk to the top of the stairs and slowly make his way down them, one step at a time, gradually getting closer to the people he loved. But as he made his way further down the stairs, the steps grew taller and more difficult to manage and as he desperately struggled his way down, one by one, he found that they were multiplying and he was moving further away from everyone. He would scream, calling his brother's names;

"Eric! Keith!"

But they couldn't hear him, they didn't even know he was there. They would never look for him and he would fall deeper and deeper into the house, further away from reality and what he knew. Trapped inside a house of which he was terrified of, with entities he had feared for most of his life. He explained that what scared him most was that when he would one day die, his ghost might return to Poultney Road with all those other trapped souls and it would be there that he'd spend eternity.

*****

When he told me about this dream, I was left speechless. It was one of the most terrifying things I think I have ever heard. Growing up in a haunted house and living a life visited by ghosts and spirits is one thing; being trapped with them for eternity is a whole new nightmare.

Chapter Fifteen

Much to the attendees' dismay, Richard did no more Ouija boards or séances. Each time he'd dabbled, it had resulted in a lot more than he'd anticipated and, once his children were involved, he knew it was time to call off the mission before anything got out of control.

The Camps carried on their lives as normal and very little paranormal activity took place between the years of 1948, when the boys were being visited by the man that Ellen would refer to as Uncle; and 1958. Electrification of the train line in South Woodford in 1947 made it still more popular and so Henry's work became busier, in an era when wages were rising dramatically, he was bringing in more money. Richard's photography grew ever more popular in 1952 when the black smog fell across London and he sold a few photographs to the local paper. Life was good for the Camps and when, in 1958, Robert was soon to turn sixteen, his parents were planning a surprise party for him. They felt that he deserved it. Birthdays weren't usually fussed over but Ellen considered this birthday to be a special one. They'd been worried when he'd dropped out of school early but when he got himself a job as an apprentice mechanic at Dove Garage in Snaresbrook, they couldn't have been prouder. He'd found something he really enjoyed and his parents were both very proud of him. However, this was because they were unaware of what had happened the day before his birthday.

*****

Being a trainee mechanic, Robert loved cars and, the same as many young boys do, had a passion for motorbikes. He had himself a Norton ES2 at home which he'd picked up from Fred's Breakers when he got his first pay packet. Although he wasn't legally allowed to ride the bike on the road, he enjoyed the challenge of restoring a tired, worn out bike to its former glory and would often spend his evenings after getting home from the garage, working on his pride and joy with his brother Eric.

He'd been working alone at the garage late one afternoon when a customer brought in his motorbike, asking for a few minor repairs to be done by Jeffrey upon his return to the body-shop the next day.

"That's fine." Robert assured him. "If you come back about lunchtime, I'm sure he'll have it finished for you."

Jeffrey was the owner of the garage but had left Robert in charge for the afternoon whilst he made some errands.

The customer handed his bike over in return for a handwritten receipt and off he went. Robert inspected the bike; it was magnificent. It was a shiny black-and-silver Douglas Dragonfly; he had often admired them from afar but had never had the chance to look at one up close before. He stood at the side of the bike for a minute or two contemplating the trouble he would get in if he was caught astride the bike, just to see how it felt. He couldn't resist and

178

jumped onto the seat, hands on the accelerator and clutch, imagining he was riding through the streets of London, everyone admiring the roar of the exhaust. It was too much for Robert to bear; he jumped off the bike, grabbed the keys from the side counter and hopped back into the driver's seat, this time pushing the key into the ignition and waiting for the engine to growl. Growl it did and, before he knew it, he'd pushed down on the accelerator and was out on the road. Feeling the wind on his face, he slowed down slightly so that he could savour the moment. He decided to pull in at home to see if his brother Eric was in from school so that he could show off his new ride.

He pulled onto Poultney Road and jumped off the bike. There was absolutely no way his parents could see him riding it, they'd keep him indoors for a year; so he locked the bike and left it at the end of the road and walked down to his house. He crept inside and went straight to his brother's room at the front of the house. He pushed open the door but the only one inside was Keith.

"Where's Eric?" Robert demanded.

"He's not home from school yet. Why?" Keith asked.

"I've got a very special secret outside, do you want to come see?" he asked his brother.

Keith nodded his head and jumped up from his bed. He was only eleven but loved spending time with his brothers and Robert had learnt that he was trustworthy and able to keep a secret, and so allowed him to join him on his adventure that afternoon. They sneaked out the front door and down the road back to the beautiful bike.

"You get on the pillar, and hold on tight, OK?" Richard said whilst getting himself comfortable; and off they went.

Richard rode the same route as he had coming, through the London roads from his house in Poultney Road back to the workshop but unfortunately, they didn't make it all the way there. About five minutes into the journey, the boys were racing cars and dodging pedal bikes when, out of nowhere, came a police car. Robert contemplated a chase but thought better of it and pulled over to the side of the road. The policeman knew Robert and had pulled him up on speeding one of his other bikes round the streets.

"Not you again, Robert. You can't keep yourself away from trouble for longer than five minutes," Constable Wickby said. "Do your parents know you're out driving this with your brother?"

"No, sir, and please don't tell them." Robert replied with elaborate politeness, "it's my birthday tomorrow sir, please, if you just give me a caution, I promise not to take anymore bikes out for a while and when I do, I'll keep to a cruising speed," he said with a wink.

Robert had a way of getting himself out of trouble, it was always the same even at school, he would end up in detention more than any of his friends but his teachers never had a bad word to say about him. He was extremely likeable.

Constable Wickby agreed to let the boys off lightly so long as they pushed the bike the rest of the way and stayed out of trouble for the foreseeable future, and that included waiting until he had a license before riding his next bike. Being just eleven, Keith was still rather impressionable and looked up to his big brother.

"Whose bike is this Robert?" he asked innocently.

"It's a friend's, but be sure not to tell anybody about it as we wouldn't want it getting back to Wickby that the bike isn't mine; OK?" Robert said, remaining cool whilst he pushed the bike out of sight of the policeman.

"OK," Keith turned to face his brother, "your secret's safe with me," returning his brother's wink.

They both burst into laughter and joked all the way back to the garage where they dropped the bike and walked back to Poultney Road.

*****

As Robert was their first child to reach sixteen, Ellen and Richard decided that they'd throw him a small party, with just few of their friends and family and a couple of Robert's friends also. Robert invited his three closest friends, James, Johnny and Gary. He'd been friends with them since he was

181

ten years old and they had grown up together and become inseparable. Besides these three friends, he loved spending time with no one more than his brother, Eric, who was a little more than a year younger, and Eric would often hang out with Robert and his friends, missing school and being mischievous, but this year Robert had really put in the effort and his parents wanted to reward him for it. Ellen and Flo made a selection of sandwiches and cakes which were all devoured by their guests, and everyone stayed until they were all danced and talked out.

Robert's friends were the last to leave and he walked them outside to send them on their way.

"I think he enjoyed himself, don't you?" Ellen asked.

"He certainly did," Richard replied, whilst washing up the dirty dishes. "I can't believe our little boy has grown up so fast."

Flo and Henry walked into the kitchen, both carrying copious amounts of dirty dishes, cutlery and empty packets.

"Mum, Dad, go up to bed. Ellen and I can take it from here." No sooner had Richard said the words than Keith ran into the kitchen, copying his grandparents and, in the process, dropped two glasses which smashed onto the kitchen floor.

"OK, that's it, everybody out," Richard demanded, ushering everyone out of the kitchen and into the family sitting room. "Leave Ellen and I to clear up; boys, go and check on your brother; Mum, Dad, go to bed, it's getting late, we'll be fine down here."

No one needed to be told twice and Ellen and Richard were left alone in the kitchen to sort out the evening's mess.

Eric and Keith made their way outside to find their brother Robert who was just down the road, still talking to Johnny. Johnny was a nice albino boy with the whitest hair and palest blue eyes you'd ever seen. Johnny never got into any trouble and kept himself to himself; the opposite of Robert, really who always seemed to be in the wrong place at the wrong time. The four boys stood round for a while, talking about school and girls and their plans for the next week. Standing on the edge of the pavement, Robert, Eric and Johnny performed their well-rehearsed handshake and split into their own directions.

The three brothers pushed through the front door to number 106 and shouted out their goodnights as they each made their way to their bedrooms. Eric and Keith were still sharing a bedroom at the front of the house whilst Robert retired to his room upstairs. As he made his way along the narrow hallway to his bedroom, he paid only cursory attention to his parents' Alsatian, Prince, making a sharp exit from his room.

"Hey, boy," he called after him but the dog didn't listen and made his way hurriedly down the stairs. He walked into his room, closing the heavy wooden door behind him. He quickly removed his clothes that he'd been wearing all day, his favourite black drainpipes, which were coated in grease from labour at the garage and a tight fitting white t-shirt tucked in. Leaving only his pants on, he climbed into bed and rested his head into his hands. He was still so fired up from the week's events; the excitement from getting to drive the Douglas Dragonfly and managing to get away without so much as a ticket from the Copper that had pulled him over, and then coming home to the excitement of his very own birthday party. Being one of the oldest in his year, he was the first of his friends to turn sixteen and hadn't been to any parties since his very first girlfriend, Valerie, had turned sixteen a few months before. It was a short-lived romance, which was also somewhat one-sided and had never made it past first-base, but one that was sweet and memorable nevertheless.

As he lay awake in bed on that very cold, dark October night, he felt himself drift into a sleep which nourished him with friends, family and non-existent lovers who would watch him ride his very own Douglas Dragonfly.

*****

It wasn't long into the night that Robert awoke. He wasn't sure what it was that had disturbed him but, unlike other nights when he woke to visit the bathroom, this time his bladder was far from full and he had no urge to visit the lavatory. He shuffled himself onto his left side so that he was facing the door at the other side of the room and lay still for a moment, willing himself to return to sleep. He could hear nothing but the sound of his own heart beating, a slow rhythmic pace that was hypnotic enough to send just about anyone to sleep, but not tonight; Robert sat up in bed and looked around. He felt as though someone was in the room with him but, with all the lights out and only a small amount of light creeping in from the deep red velvet curtains, he wasn't able to see much of anything. He blinked ferociously trying to adjust his eyes in the dark and, as he did, he noticed that there was a figure standing at the bottom of him bed.

"Mum? Dad?" he spoke aloud to what looked like the outline of a person standing with their back to him, facing the wardrobe at the bottom of his bed.

Still in a dreamlike state, Robert could only think that it wasn't as late as he thought and his Mum had come into his room to collect his washing in time for the morning.

"Mum is that you? You woke me," he said.

The figure didn't move but he noticed that she had long, light hair, just like Ellen, and so he laid back into his pillow and relaxed, believing the figure was no-one to fear and was just, in fact, his mother.

"Mum, you scared me." He lay still for a moment and waited for some kind of response, "What's taking you so long?" he asked as he sat up against his headboard, rubbing his eyes and wandering what   on earth Ellen was doing.

As he sat up and observed the woman, she very slowly turned to face him. The room was still very dark but the woman stood out as she was dressed in a long, light grey translucent robe which clashed with the darkness of the mahogany coloured wardrobe behind her. As he considered this woman's attire, it suddenly struck him that he'd never seen his mother wear something so erotic and considered the likelihood that she would even want her sons to see her walking around on a cold winter's night, baring most of her body beneath her night dress. Still unable to focus too much on what was in front of him, Robert pinched himself to ensure he wasn't dreaming. His mother had long blonde hair but, as he moved himself further down the bed, and towards this apparition that was now making her way towards the lower end of his bed Robert could see that this woman's hair wasn't blonde but a white shade of grey, and he could now see that this woman was nothing like his mother. Her grey hair was much longer, and straw-like, which covered the bareness of her buttocks beneath her nightdress and her small bosom was less proud than that of Ellen's, whose motherly figure bore no resemblance whatsoever to the wafer-thin woman who was standing in front of him, getting closer as each second passed.

Robert hadn't experienced much of what his other brothers had previously, and had been sheltered from the secrets that number 106 Poultney Road had within its walls. He had, from time to time, noticed that each evening he'd see his father close the cupboard door on the landing outside his bedroom and lock it with a key he kept in his room, only to find the door open again each morning with no sign of the key which must have been used to open it. He'd always put that down to his father's carelessness and never thought that it could be anything sinister. He didn't even know whether he believed in life after death or the rumours that had spread around his school about the house that he lived in but, tonight, it would seem that those rumours were going to be proved true.

Robert, transfixed his eyes on the woman that moved in front of him, closed them and rubbed them vigorously. He couldn't believe what he was witnessing. He pulled his knees into his chest and desperately tried to scream, to call for help from anyone but it was as though his entire body had frozen with fear and he couldn't find his voice, although he searched hard. So he sat still and silent, with his eyes tightly closed, hoping that when he re-opened them the ghostly image would disappear. He counted to three in his head and opened his eyes. The woman was gone; no longer at the end of his bed, nor near his wardrobe. Just as he drew in a long, deep breath of relief, he suddenly felt a soft, stroking sensation on the back of his neck. Slowly, and without any sudden movement, Robert turned his face to meet the sensation and there she was; standing next to him, head hung over him. Without being able to fight it, his body collapsed and he let go of his knees as the phantom woman leaned her head over his, allowing her long, grey hair to coat his face, brushing past his own head of thick, brown locks. He looked up seeking her eyes, trying to discover who she could be but, to Robert's horror, he saw that her face bore no features. There were closed sockets where her eyes should be; a small mound in place of her nose and just a smooth enclosed crevice in place of her mouth. He could see that the skin which covered her tiny body and face was so thin and fragile that he was able to see the bones pressing, painfully, through the membrane, like a broken bone would protrude through an open wound. The only difference was that there was no wound; no flesh and no muscle to cut through, just a skeletal frame with no substance.

With all of his might, Robert pulled himself from beneath the woman, and somersaulted himself to the bottom of the bed, falling to the floor where he scrambled his way to the other side of the room, in the opposite corner to the door. He sat in sheer disbelief, watching the actions of the ghost, or apparition or whatever it is you'd want to call her. He watched as she turned to face the wardrobe at the end of the bed and she slowly made her way back, up to the cupboard where she spread her gaunt, emaciated arms, leant back into the wood and disappeared.

It was only then that Robert managed to pick himself up and run screaming from his bedroom, down the stairs and out through the front door. He never even gave himself time to grab clothes; he just wanted to get out and away from whoever it was that had visited him that night. He ran all the way to his friend Johnny's house, six streets away. Luckily, no one saw him as he would probably have been arrested for indecent exposure, but he wouldn't have cared. He swore blind that he'd never re-enter his old bedroom and true to his word, he never did.

He explained to his parents what had happened that night and, much to his surprise, they believed him with very little questioning. It was then that Richard decided that by them ignoring the paranormal activity that was taking place within the house wouldn't make it go away, as he had left it alone for ten years. He and Ellen decided to resume the investigations they'd started years before.

Chapter Sixteen

A new decade dawned and the Camps, like many others, benefited from the fresh vibrancy it brought, each of them comfortably finding their place in the society that was evolving around them. The one thing that hadn't altered, and never would, was the house in which they lived; the building which encompassed all of their hopes and dreams, fears and nightmares; the house on Poultney Road. Robert had never gone into too much detail about that night to anyone but his parents; he especially didn't dramatise it in front of his youngest brother, Keith. It had been a horrific experience that he was happy to forget or, at least, push to the back of his mind. One thing that became obvious over the years was that it wasn't the people living on Poultney Road that were haunted; it was the house itself. Months would often pass without any disturbances happening to the family, only the minor incidents like the creaking of floor-boards, or the sound of people crying in the night, that simply became part of every-day life in the Camp household.

The months passed and soon became years and, on the Eve of Dec 31, 1962, Eric was celebrating his sixteenth birthday. It wasn't quite as eventful as Robert's sixteenth had been but Eric was pleased with it. He'd grown into a very caring young man and had become quite a hit with the ladies, always having a pretty young girl on his arm. A few months after he'd left his childhood behind and turned sixteen, he decided to take the plunge and ask a girl out he'd been eager to date for a while. Her name was Tracy and, with long red

191

hair, dimpled checks and a tiny waist, she was the envy of every girl in her class and by bagging himself a date with her, Eric was outright admired by all of his mates. He surprised her by taking her to see The Curse of the Werewolf. Eric loved nothing more than a Hammer horror for trying his luck with the ladies, and it didn't run short with Tracy. With plenty of mutilation and the usual, helpless damsel in distress, Eric was able to get himself a little closer to his date, demonstrating the endless charm of the stretch-arms-out-and-around-the-shoulder move which worked every time, and even this time it didn't fail to get him a snog in the back row.

Being the gentleman that he was, Eric walked Tracy home, she didn't live far from him and it meant he was able to squeeze in that all-important kiss goodnight. He left the young girl a million miles away on her doorstep, in awe of the boy who'd just stolen her first kiss, watching him swagger down the end of her road, looking back only to blow a kiss in her direction.

"Gotcha," he smiled to himself as he turned the corner.

Eric may have been a charmer and a ladies' man, but his heart was in the right place; he just hadn't yet found the right woman to tame him.

When he turned his key in the lock, he knew it must be late as he'd seen the late showing of the movie which must have finished soon after eleven o'clock. Gone midnight and his parents in bed, he gently opened the front door and removed the key as he closed it behind him. He still shared a room with his younger brother, Keith; they were used to the other one coming in and out like they lived in a hotel. They loved to sit up sharing stories but tonight, as Eric made his way into the bedroom, the lights were out and Keith was asleep. As he turned to close the bedroom door behind him he could hear the floorboards upstairs, creaking. Although he was used to this, it still didn't stop him from hesitating for a moment before reassuring himself that the house was getting old and that, just like people, houses could become a bit cranky. As he turned to close the door, he heard the creaking again but, this time, the scraping was repetitive and sounded as though it was coming from upstairs, towards the back of the house. He raised himself onto tiptoe and stepped quietly across the hall to the bottom of the stairs. He stood very still for a moment and listened.

"Nan? Granddad?" he called and waited for one of them to reply, but they didn't so much as stir.

He lifted one of his muscular calves and placed his barefoot on the first stair, listening with every movement. Then he heard it again. A creaking, rickety sound; as though something or someone was rolling across the wooden floor in the back bedroom, the one that Eric's grandparents used as their sitting room. It then dawned on Eric that it must be either Flo or Henry, awake and sitting in Henry's rocking chair. It wouldn't be the first time he'd found them awake in the middle of the night, wandering the halls or retiring in the sitting room, unable to sleep and blaming it on the other one's snoring. This thought eased his nerves, and the fear he'd initially felt disappeared slightly. He picked up his pace and reached the top stair, where he was then able to hear the sound of his grandparents' consistent breathing, asleep in their beds. It was a deep breathing, so it must be one of them unable to sleep in the sitting room that he was able to hear in there now. He stood momentarily as he listened; in, out. In, out. In, in, out, out. He heard two sets of breathing coming from his grandparents' room. Both of them asleep in their bed. Neither of them awake and neither of them sitting in their rocking chair in the sitting room, yet Eric could hear the unnerving sound growing louder and faster as he made his way towards the wooden door which separated him from whatever was awake inside that room.

He crept his way over and placed his smaller-than-average ear against the cold, solid wooden door; as he did, the noise appeared to be banging its way through the fibres, absorbing its way into his head; over and over; louder and louder and then silence. As if simultaneously with his hand reaching for the door handle, the commotion that had been coming from within the room stopped. Eric stopped in his tracks and lifted his hand away from the cold, brass handle and hesitated slightly for just a moment until curiosity won the battle and he took the plunge, grabbed the handle and pushed down with utter certainty; eager to know what or who it was, playing with his emotions. As the door flew open, he was hit by a freezing chill that seemed to brush through his body and, as it did, he saw the room was in darkness with only a small amount of light coming in from the station, through the trees that stood tall at the end of the garden. The light allowed enough for him to see that the room was empty and everything was still. For a moment Eric doubted himself, considering that what he just heard had been a figment of his imagination. It was late and he had a lot on his mind, perhaps it was time he took himself to bed, he thought. As he turned on his heel, feeling a little sheepish, he felt the atmosphere in the room change. He froze in his tracks as the density submerged him and his feet became too heavy to move. It started again, the rolling motion that he was now certain was his grandfather's rocking chair, the one that was behind him and apparently empty. It started as a slow, gradual movement but as Eric found it in him to turn his head and face the mysterious commotion, the rocking became furious and the sound of wood against wood was almost too loud to bear. Eric managed to turn his head and his body soon followed but before he'd turned fully, he felt a pressure against his chest as the words:

"GO BACK TO BED!"

were yelled by a visionless man, positioned close to or actually sitting in, the rocking chair that was now rocking so fast that Eric was afraid that it may burst through the boards or, worse still, the ceiling.

He didn't wait around to see what might happen, Eric ran out of the room as fast as his legs would carry him, jumped into bed and hid his head below the duvet which is how he woke the following morning.

"You alright in there, Eric?" Keith asked, pulling at Eric's quilt. "You're lucky you didn't suffocate, sleeping under there all night."

Chapter Seventeen

Henry was sick. The Camps knew it and so did he if he'd admit it. It was a trait of the family that illness was something they'd hide until they had no choice but to make a trip to the doctor. When Eric wasn't much older than eleven, he and Robert took Keith to the forests to climb trees, play football and generally do what young boys do, but poor Keith took a tumble and snapped the radius in his left arm. Being his left arm and not his right, he was able to hide it well and keep it from his parents for three days; that was, until it swelled so much that he wasn't able to fit it through the armhole of any of his jumpers. Of course his brothers teased him for being a 'big girl' for telling his Mum, but it was lucky he did as the doctors were only just able to set it straight.

But Henry was different, he'd always been a man who enjoyed being busy, he was never one to sit and watch others without getting involved but, over the course of a month or so, he'd slowed down, he was sleeping longer and moving more slowly. Flo was concerned and asked what was wrong, but he made light of his frail condition. Henry wasn't old but he wasn't getting any younger, and looking after one another in a relationship becomes second nature to most couples, and so it did with Flo and Henry. However, it wasn't long before Richard, Ellen and the boys noticed that there was something wrong. He'd started skipping meals and his weight plummeted; he lost interest in current affairs and in those around him. Henry seldom complained about anything and didn't make his family aware of any discomfort that he was in but was in fact, covering up an excruciating pain that was developing in his stomach and digestive system, the vomiting that he experienced whenever he ate, and the fresh blood that he'd begun to throw up. At just sixty years old, in March 1963, Henry Camp died from stomach cancer, which was killing him from the inside out. His death hit his family hard and for a while they couldn't bring themselves to even speak about the man that had driven their family forwards for so many years. Richard soon became the man of the house, providing for his family and looking after their needs.

It wasn't long before Richard, again, delved in the paranormal. He and his family were becoming used to the cries in the night, the locking and unlocking of cupboard doors and footsteps on the floorboards and, this time, it wasn't the man in black or his childhood friend that pulled his attention back to the dead; it was the possibility of contacting his father. He'd been doing more research, talking to people when he was at work or having a pint, at the Old Bell, before reaching his own conclusion. Although it was possible that he was only going to contact evil when he reached out to spirits using Ouija boards and séances, there was the possibility that he may contact a good spirit and one which wanted to help lost souls. He came to the realisation that what he was able to do was in fact a gift and that he shouldn't hide from it. He could use it to his advantage, try to speak to his father and ensure that his spirit rested on the other side and, if he wasn't able to contact him directly, then he should be able to put to rest anything that he was able to communicate with. He'd obviously connected with something by accident when he was younger that had stayed with him and his family in that house, and over time it was presenting itself to every member and so he decided that by contacting something good, maybe even his late father, the goodness in him would possibly overcome the evil that haunted his house. He believed that perhaps, in doing this, the bad soul would eventually be able to rest in peace.

He hadn't discussed his theories with Ellen as he wasn't sure how she would take them but it wasn't something he was going to be able to hide from her and so decided to bring it to light one bright, sunny afternoon in July 1963. He'd asked her to meet him at Hyde Park Corner station after work for a stroll around Hyde Park. It was the perfect weather for an evening stroll and there wasn't going to be a better time to tell his wife such news. People generally seemed to take bad, or slightly absurd, news better when the sun was shining, and Ellen was no exception. They met on time, shared a brief kiss and started on their way.

"You couldn't have chosen a better evening for this Richard. It's really nice of you to have suggested some time to ourselves. It feels like we never get private time anymore. When you're not busy at work or out at the Old Bell, we are busy at home. I forget about us sometimes," Ellen said as they made their way through the gates into the lush greenery of the park.

There was never going to be a good time to break the news, but Richard felt comforted by the lush greenery and beauty that surrounded him; they seemed like a million miles away from the fears that hid in their home.

"Ellen, I need to speak to you," he said hesitantly.

"This sounds ominous," his wife replied.

Richard stood for a moment.

"Let's take a seat," he suggested, whilst guiding his wife to a wooden bench which, he noted, had the remembrance words engraved on a plaque:

Taken too early,

You were just 47.

God must have wanted you,

With him up in heaven.

Joseph Braker

1912 – 1959

He shook the image of death from his brain and continued to think of the best way to break the news to his wife that he wanted to take up séance hosting once again.

"Richard what is it? What's wrong? You're scaring me," Ellen pleaded.

"Don't be silly, I'm making this seem a lot worse than it is," he explained. "Losing Dad hit me hard; it hit us all hard and it got me thinking." He paused considering how to say what he had to.

"Go on..." Ellen begged.

"OK. I want to try a séance again," he blurted out.

Ellen stood to her feet. "Are you joking?" she said raising her voice. "After everything that's happened you want to play again with the devil!" she shouted.

"No sweetheart, it's not like that. Sit down, let me explain," Richard said trying to reassure his wife, eager for her to sit down and let him explain. "I don't see that we've ever, really been threatened by any ghosts; nothing has come to hurt us."

"Are you joking? I don't have to listen to this," Ellen said, jumping straight back onto her feet. "You don't call your child being attacked by a disappearing man or your other children being stalked by other spirits threatening?" Ellen asked incredulously.

"I'm not saying that, but what I am saying is that these could just be a cry for help. It could be their way of telling us that they need help," he said whilst taking his wife's hand. "Sit down and let me finish," he asked, and Ellen did. "It's not only that but it could be possible for me to contact Dad and it would put my mind at ease to know that he's OK and he's no longer suffering."

As he looked down at his feet and felt his eyes fill with water, he felt the reassuring touch of his wife's hand on the back of his neck. He looked up to meet her eyes.

"I understand," she said. "You don't have to explain, I understand."

With that he turned and wrapped his arms around Ellen's neck and thanked her. It meant so much to him that he would have her on his side. Her support had been his strength over the years, she acted as his rock, and knowing that she was on his side about this encouraged him to want to make it work more than he did already. They stayed on that bench for almost two hours, smoking cigarettes and talking about the past and the future.

*****

It wasn't long before word got out and the usual group were ready for their next gathering. Richard had told all of the family what he intended to do and explained that using Ouija boards and séances was the only way to connect with the spirits that had resided in their home. Perhaps because they had grown accustomed to it, all of them were fine and Keith, who was sixteen, wanted to be involved himself. Richard agreed to let him participate in the first vigil, but only as a spectator; he didn't want any of his children to be at risk. It was on August 17th that the first meeting took place but unlike the last time, there were only six attendees, plus Keith. Involved were Margaret, Paul, Juliet, Frank, Phyllis and Richard. Mike had passed away in December the previous year and so Phyllis was keen to make contact with him. As he hadn't held one of these gatherings for a few years, he wanted to ease himself in slowly and thought that this would be a good way to make it more personal and less likely to get out of hand, especially as his son was a spectator on the far side of the room.

Everyone arrived, as before, at eight o'clock and the front room upstairs was prepared. One by one they made their way to the second storey of the house and positioned themselves around the room. Waiting for everyone to arrive, there was small talk among them and shortly after the last person arrived, Frank began to tell the others about a recurring dream he'd been having.

"I experienced it for the first time last week," he began, "I've never suffered from nightmares or terrors in the past and so this one took me by surprise. It started with me inside this house, I don't know why I was here or why I had an urgent need to escape," Frank explained. "I felt suffocated inside the walls, gasping for air as it was escaping my lungs. I pushed my way through the front door. Now I don't know why I remember some things and other things I seem to forget when I wake up, but I remember that outside it was cold and black. There was barely any light coming from anywhere but the moon. In my dream I can remember feeling confused and very disorientated and as I looked up

203

and down the road, I was drawn to the light coming from the end of Poultney Road so I turn and run to the right of the house, away from number 106 and seemingly away from the darkness. However, no sooner do I run, than the darkness follows me. The bulbs in the street lamps smash one by one the further I get from the house. Like the darkness is chasing me; like the house is following me." Frank looked at his attentive listeners, then continued, "It's as though I'm running from something but I don't know what. It always gets darker the further from the house I run and the air becomes heavy, making it difficult to breathe. Part of me always wants to return to this house in my dream, but something pushes me on, further into the darkness, slowly being absorbed by the blackness."

Everyone, including Richard, was listening to Frank's every word, eager to know where he would end up.

"I don't know if you have dreams like it but this dream, or nightmare, whichever you want to call it, always seems to change and instead of me running down the open road, as I get closer to the end of what seems to be a never ending street, it changes so that it feels more like an enclosed space, a tunnel perhaps, creeping in around me, capturing me and as it does, so the oxygen that I am desperately trying to inhale, is getting denser and more difficult to absorb."

He paused momentarily, "Come on, don't leave us hanging," Juliet beseeched.

"Sorry, Juliet, it's just that the end of my dream frightens me so much, I find it hard to retell. You see, the whole time I'm running, there's light in front of me, giving me hope as I leave the darkness behind me but when I get to where I strive to be, the end of the tunnel, the street opens up and I'm alone inside a field; a large empty field of nothingness with only minimal light shining into it from the moon above me. I look behind me, terrified, not knowing where I am and nothing guiding me to where I want to go, when I find that there is no air left to breathe, nothing keeping the blood in my veins moving, the air in my lungs circulating and as I fall to my knees, gasping for breath, the light from the moon drops. Pitch black." He stopped.

"And?" Richard asked.

"And nothing, I always wake up, in my bed, or wherever I may have fallen asleep, alone in my house. There's never anything sinister when I wake up but, I tell you, these dreams are so real, so terrifying, that I find it hard to catch my breath when I wake. It really frightens me and what terrifies me the most is that it happened for the third time last night and when I made my way to the bedroom from the sofa where I woke, I noticed bloody prints following me. When I looked down at my feet, the soles were covered in mud and one of them had a small stone embedded inside it, bleeding. You don't think it could be some kind of outer-body experience, do you? People say that it's possible you know."

205

No-one had anything to say in response to his question. None of them had any experiences of their own or words of wisdom to offer this man who had confided in them. Keith, more than anyone else, was terrified.

Richard let go of the silence and suggested moving onto the night's séance.

"If we can all join hands and make a circle, I'd like to start with the evening's main focus." And with that, he began chanting as he'd done before, this time however, he was more confident, unafraid of what may happen or who he would contact, as he felt that whoever or whatever it may be would have a purpose.

"If anyone's there give us a sign, if anyone's there, give us a sign." Richard asked.

Everyone joined in with the chanting. As they had once before, nothing happened for a while, it seemed like hours passed and in fact, almost thirty minutes did before anything happened. Keith, not knowing any different, thought that the night had been a shambles. Then it started. Initially he felt a chill that filled the room and a breeze which gushed past them all one by one. They all looked above their heads as the dim light began to flicker.

"No-one break the chain, keep holding onto the person's hand next to you, tightly." Richard requested as he squeezed Paul's hand a little tighter.

As he did, the sound of planes in the distance filled their ears. None of them were entirely sure what the noise was to begin with, but it grew louder and more obvious that the sound was of a fighter plane. They all listened in silence as the roar of the plane's engine grew closer and louder. Keith, who was standing motionless in the corner of the room, watched the events unfold and was amazed by what he witnessed. Although he'd experienced the paranormal before, he'd never been involved in anything that was so obviously real; there was nothing that could deny the situation he was in. Nothing and no-one could argue otherwise. Regardless of its likelihood, it was happening.

"What is that?" Margaret asked.

"Impossible, that's what it is," Frank replied. "I never fought in the First World War but I would recognise that aircraft from miles away." He shouted, in an attempt to be heard above the roar of the engine. "It's a Vickers FB5 Gunbus. One of the first fighter planes to take to the skies in the First World War. There's no way there'd be one in the skies tonight. That noise isn't coming from anything that exists in this day and age, those planes haven't flown in years; there's no purpose for them now." He turned to face Richard, "Richard, is there such thing as a ghost plane? Surely not?" he shouted. "You're the host, what do we do?"

His question was a loud cry, as they all began to duck, the sound of the roaring plane giving the distinct impression it was about to come crashing through the walls of the house.

The windows shuddered with the vibrations. Everyone dropped down to their knees and, without letting go of each other's hands, crawled beneath the table. Although impossible, none of them were willing to risk the invasion being real. Then, as if hearing their silent prayers, the plane sounded as though it was lifting above the height of the house, and flew right over - leaving the host and his séance attendees shrivelled up on the floor like dishevelled bodies whose lives had been taken and their bodies dumped.

*****

No-one had wanted to continue after what they'd experienced and they decided to call it a night. Keith had been the most disturbed by the event as he'd watched from outside the circle, able to see and hear everything and he, too, had ended the experience by seeking shelter underneath the table. After everyone had left, he followed his father downstairs and into the kitchen where he sat at the dining table and waited for his Dad to prepare him a hot cup of tea.

"Has that happened before?" he asked Richard who was busying himself round the kitchen.

"By 'that' I presume you mean the plane?" Keith nodded. "No, it hasn't but that's not to say that I haven't experienced worse."

Keith was quiet for a minute.

"Why do you think it happens? Do you think it's this house? That it somehow draws in evil? Or," he paused, "do you think that the spirits are attracted to you?"

Richard stopped what he was doing, spoon in mid-stir. His son's words had hit a nerve, perhaps because it was something he'd always considered himself but never wanted to accept. He'd always blamed the house; it was easy to call a house haunted, but to be the haunted was an entirely different scenario.

"I don't know," he answered his son honestly. "I wouldn't like to think that it's the second of the two options but it seems the first is more plausible.

Richard slung back his cup of hot tea that he'd purposely filled with cold milk and told his son he wanted to go to bed.

"You should do the same. Don't think about it too much, it'll play havoc with your dreams," Richard said as he left the kitchen and made his way upstairs to bed.

Keith didn't sit for long, he couldn't finish his tea, the milk wouldn't settle, he could feel it curdling around in his stomach. The evening had left a sour taste in his mouth, he still felt dizzy from the night's events and he thought that bed would be the best place for him. It wasn't long before midnight that he retired to his room. Alone tonight without Eric sleeping in there too, he climbed under the duvet and drifted off to sleep.

He couldn't breathe, he gasped for breath as his lungs contracted but to no avail. It took Keith a moment to adjust to the shock that had hit his system. He was awake, it wasn't a dream, he knew that much for sure but, how or what was happening he'd no idea. As he came to his senses, he realised the reason why he wasn't able to breathe. Someone had their hands around his throat and was strangling him. Someone was trying to kill him. It was dark in the room but his eyes were adjusting quickly; however he couldn't see anyone standing over him. He fought against the strength of the murderous hands around his neck, and could positively testify to their existence but why wasn't he able to see anyone? As his eyes adjusted further he could see someone was standing to the left of his bed. It was hard for him to concentrate on anything but fighting for his life, but he visualised another figure that was watching over the whole thing. It was a man dressed in a brown uniform. He looked very dapper, with a brown bomber-style jacket and beige-brown baggy trousers which were tucked into knee-length buckle boots. As Keith struggled and threw his body high and head forwards, he caught sight of the man's face. Hidden beneath an aviator helmet and goggles, Keith saw something which literally took his breath away, and left him momentarily stunned. Beneath the mysterious man's attire was a face that had quite clearly been blown to pieces with the left-hand side of it ripped right off, with his left ear and cheek replaced by a mushy mess of red pulp and blue veins.

His eye had prolapsed and was resting on the open chaos where his cheek should have been. As Keith focused on the apparition in front of him, thinking that he'd be the last thing he was going to see before he died, the fighter pilot standing clearly in front of him took a shotgun from his pocket, pointed to where the invisible presence was lurking over Keith, and pulled the trigger.

Keith had closed his eyes; half-shocked, half-exhausted and lying dormant for what seemed like an eternity but couldn't have been more than twenty seconds. His rapid breathing slowly returned to normal and he was able to regain his composure before sitting upright in his bed. He looked around the room, eager for some evidence of the two apparitions that had been with him in his room. For the imperceptible phantom which had been trying so desperately to kill him and for the man who had scared him half to death but then saved his life. But there was no evidence of either. The room was empty and he was alone. It was as if nothing had ever happened, but Keith knew it had and, no doubt, his father would too when he told him.

As he lay in bed, he thought about the terror that had occurred over and over in his mind, and then the connection suddenly came to him. Earlier that night, in the séance, they'd been terrorised by the sound of a fighter plane and now, he'd been attacked by someone who looked like they could have been flying that plane fifty years ago.

What has Dad got himself into? he thought. For Keith knew that now there was no turning back and that his Dad had opened a gateway to another world when he conducted the séance, as he would every time he did another.

He wondered whether his Dad knew this already and whether it was in fact what he wanted.

*****

Sadly, two weeks after the telling of his recurring dream, Frank died in circumstances not dissimilar to those he detailed on the night of the séance. He was walking home one night from church when he suffered a heart attack on the cold streets of London, alone and in the dark.

Chapter Eighteen

From that night on, Richard held a séance or Ouija board at Poultney Road on a monthly basis. The same mix of people came and, every time, they'd contact a different soul that Richard believed was either lost or in need of some resolution. It took him five or six months to realise that each time he contacted someone new, his theory of good overcoming evil didn't seem to work. His idea that by contacting a good presence and then a dangerous, or rather confused, one, the good spirit would help the evil one rest or find some kind of light at the end of the tunnel; however, ghosts didn't come with a label and there weren't good or bad spirits, but instead, all were souls that were lost in limbo. Whether this was because they were killed suddenly or because they were attached to someone who was still living and wouldn't let go of ties they had on earth, it seemed that once Richard connected with any of them, it was then impossible to help them. This meant one thing; that number 106 Poultney Road was becoming crowded.

Eric was now twenty and working on his own fruit and veg stall in the local market. Surrounding him were other traders selling delicacies, clothing and disposable goods, all of whom made a decent living. He'd learnt from his father how to be a hard grafter and Eric was proving to be a good student. He had a lot of regulars and, yes, he often greeted them in the stereotypical market stall trader manner;

"Hello lovely ladies, get yourself some of my perfectly ripe fresh fruit and veg. Give your husband something to smile about when he gets home and have the tastiest veg waiting on his plate."

The women loved it. The queue would trail up the road as far as the eye could see. Eric had always been a success with the ladies and he seemed to have a different woman on his arm every week. He was known around the area for being a bit of a ladies' man and, secretly, he loved his reputation. That was until he saw her.

It was a steaming hot day in July 1964 and Eric was busier than usual on the stall. In the two hours he'd been open, he'd taken more than he would usually during an entire weekend of trading. With the sun shining and more people on the street than usual, he knew it was going to be a good day for business. It was when he was saying goodbye to one of his most regular customers, Mrs Grimsby - a tall, rather skinny woman in her late fifties who enjoyed a bit of attention from a good-looking lad more than half her age, who walked away on this occasion with more apples and oranges than she was able to carry - that he first saw Yvonne Mynard. She was dressed more like an actress on the big screen than someone you'd expect to see walking through a London market. She was wearing a calf-length, skin-tight pale pink skirt which pinched in around the knees, a fitted matching jacket which sat over a silky, cream blouse. Her long, jet-black hair fell in curls over her shoulders and her smoky dark eyes enhanced the sexy siren image she so easily projected. A perfect size ten, this young woman was beyond Eric's standards by a mile but this only made him want her more. Although he was desperate to know her name, the stall was too busy to leave and he lost sight of the dark-haired beauty, concentrating instead on a slightly less attractive woman who was standing in front of him with a handful of cash.

The next morning, at about the same time, Eric saw her again. This time he noticed that she was walking alongside an older man - he definitely wasn't her husband, was more than likely her father - as she made her way to the station. The presence of her father made it difficult for Eric to find the gumption to approach her, so watched her walk by yet again. It was later that afternoon when he was packing up that he heard heels tapping past his stall and, to his surprise, it was her; the mysterious beauty. He dropped the mound of apples he had in his arms and followed her, at a slow enough pace not to be caught. When she reached the end of the road, he saw that the same man, her father, was waiting for her in a very shiny black Jaguar E-Type. She climbed inside without acknowledging Eric and they made off down the road. Before he had time to think the situation through, Eric turned on his heel and ran up Trenton Road and down Poultney Road to his house. Jumped on his blue and silver, Greeve Hawkstone motorbike and got on the beauty's trail.

He followed her out of London and along winding, country roads. He didn't worry about being seen as he always made sure he was just far enough behind that he wouldn't get caught. They crossed over a narrow bridge which was only

215

wide enough for a small car or, conveniently, a motorbike. All the cottages and smaller houses were out of sight and all that surrounded Eric now were huge five or six-bed homes that were, by his standards, mansions. He observed a glorious house to his left which was built from beautiful white brick and stood so tall he had to raise his head to view its entirety.

"How the other half live," he said to himself as he returned his attention to the road ahead.

As he did, he braked suddenly. He'd lost them.

"What the hell!" he said aloud as his eyes skimmed his surroundings.

He jumped off his bike and let it rest on the ground as he ran up and down the street, desperately searching for the Jag he'd somehow managed to lose sight of. And then he saw her. The car had pulled up outside a magnificent house with a plaque on an outside pillar, standing proud next to a large black gate, displaying the name SANDOWN. He wouldn't forget the house - how could he? It was amazing and better than most hotels he'd stayed in. He skipped over to his bike and rode his way back to London. Now he knew where she lived, it would be easy.

*****

He followed her home a few more times, sometimes she got the bus but most times her father would collect her. He wasn't sure but he guessed that she was going to and from college or work each day. Judging by the house she lived in and the way she dressed, he presumed she would be well educated. He knew that he would have to introduce himself at some point but he couldn't bring himself to do it just yet. The timing had to be perfect. He started to leave gifts on her doorstep when he followed her home. He always left a card with just The woman of my dreams written on a little card. He'd get the flowers off his mate, Peter, who owned a pitch next to his on the market so they were always massive bouquets which he knew would make an impression. After about a month of following her, he went home and spoke to Ellen.

"I want to take you out tonight, Mum," he said, as he helped Ellen unpack some of the groceries he'd brought in with him.

"Oh, really," she replied, "where to?"

"I'm going to show you the house which the woman lives in that I'm going to marry," he said and ran upstairs to change.

Eric had always been a man's man. He was close to both his brothers and had loads of friends who he spent most of his time with. He had plenty of girlfriends but never ones that he liked enough to introduce to his parents so when he made such a rash statement to his mum, she was shocked to say the least. He wasn't a hopeless romantic who threw "I love you's" away with the wind; to say what he had, Ellen knew he must be serious about her, whoever she was.

They left the house at eight o'clock when the evening was drawing in and they made their way on the same route that Eric had travelled the last ten nights, at least. As always he took a bouquet of flowers with him and when they arrived outside the gates, he pointed up to the house.

"See. Mum, she lives there and although I've never even spoken to this woman, I'm going to marry her. I have to," he said with conviction.

"Oh, you are funny Eric," Ellen retorted. "I want to see how serious you are. If you really want to be with this girl, I want you to deliver the flowers yourself this evening, no cheating."

"Fine," Eric replied. "You stay here. Don't move," he demanded as he pulled himself off the bike, leaving Ellen keeping her balance on the back.

He hadn't thought about getting through the gates but, as he approached them, he found that they weren't locked so he pushed his way through, made his way up the drive, took a deep breath and knocked on the large, wooden front door. He stood for a while waiting, he could feel the sweat building up on his forehead and then he heard a lock turn from the inside.

Oh no, he thought, they're in!

The door opened and in front of him stood a very petite woman, no taller than five feet and no larger than a size six. A stunning older woman whom he instantly recognised as the mother of the woman he'd fixated on; they both had the same, striking green eyes.

"Can I help you?" she asked in a very kind, warm tone.

"Yes," Eric managed, "I wonder if I can speak to the other young lady who lives here? I have some flowers for her."

"So you're the mystery florist," the little lady joked, "I'll just see if I can find her."

She left Eric standing there, closing the door in front of him. He stood on the porch for what seemed like forever and he imagined what his mum must be thinking as she sat outside, waiting on his bike. All of a sudden, the door reopened and this time, standing in front of him was the woman he'd been dying to see. She looked absolutely stunning. She was wearing a tight-fitting pair of pale denim jeans, with a pastel green chiffon blouse hanging loosely over the top. Her long, dark hair was tied into a ponytail which revealed still more of the beauty of her face.

"Can I help you?" she asked in a way that said, get to the point.

"Hi, my name's Eric. I wanted to give you these," he said as he handed her the flowers. "By the way, what's your name?"

"So it's you, the guy who's been following me. Don't let my dad see you, he thinks you're a weirdo too," she said without a change in her expression. "My name's Yvonne. It's nice to finally know who you are but honestly, I have studying I need to be getting on with. Another time maybe."

"Another time, when?" Eric interjected. "When can I take you out?"

Yvonne just stood, holding the edge of the door with every intention of shutting it firmly.

"Saturday, I guess?" she answered.

"So I can take you out Saturday?"

Yvonne nodded in agreement.

"Great, I'll pick you up about seven?"

"Fine," she replied. "But I hope you don't intend on picking me up on that motorbike you've been following me on every day; there's no way my father would allow that. I suggest that if you want to take me out, you get yourself a car."

And with that she closed the door in Eric's face. It was as if he hadn't heard the last thing she said to him as his smile stretched from ear to ear.

*****

Saturday soon arrived and Eric watched the clock until it turned six-thirty and he could head over to Yvonne's house. In the summer of 1964, Eric was very much a Mod. He wore his best grey suit with matching, fitted waistcoat and a crisp white shirt underneath. His trousers sat about an inch from his shiny, black-and-white Italian shoes, which set off his bright yellow socks. He always dressed well, but this particular date night, he needed to impress. He'd borrowed his mate's Sunbeam Talbot. It drove well, looked smart and, indeed, it wasn't a motorbike.

He arrived ten minutes early and sat waiting outside, he didn't want to get off on the wrong foot for not allowing her time to be ready. He waited until just before seven o'clock and walked over to the door and knocked. Her mum answered the door once again but this time she welcomed him into her home.

"My name's Elsie," she said cordially, "wait a moment and I'll go see if she's ready."

No sooner had Elsie left the room than Yvonne's father entered. He was a tall man and well-built. He clearly kept himself fit. His skin was dark and so too were his eyes which lead Eric to believe he was either Spanish or Italian. He looked quite scary.

"I'm Mervyn, Yvonne's father. It's nice to finally meet you, Eric," this imposing figure of a man said as he gestured towards him and held out his hand to shake his.

221

"It's a pleasure to meet you, sir," Eric replied, "thank you for letting me take your daughter out this evening."

"About that," Mervyn said. "Where do you intend to take her, and wherever it is, I want her home by nine-thirty. No later. If she walks through that door a minute late, it'll be the last time you see her. Understood?"

"Understood. I'm taking her to the Majestic cinema in South Woodford where I live and, of course, I will have her home before nine-thirty," agreed Eric who was now feeling quite intimidated.

Before long Elsie returned to the room and was followed by Yvonne, who looked immaculate. With her blue-black hair pulled high into a bun and wearing a gorgeous royal blue chiffon mini-skirt with classic cream heels, Eric had to lift his chin off the floor without Mervyn seeing him drool.

The date went smoothly besides a few hiccups; a leak in the ceiling of the cinema and a failed arm-around-the-shoulder attempt which, before that night, had worked a treat every time. Although the night didn't run smoothly, Eric had a feeling he would be seeing this girl again and, when he kissed her hand goodnight on the doorstep at nine twenty that night, he'd already arranged their next date.

Chapter Nineteen

A week passed and it was date night once again.

"When are we going to meet her?" Robert asked. "This one sounds like she's for keeps."

"Yes, I think she could be which is exactly why I don't want to scare her off too soon." Eric joked.

Robert grinned. "Come on, your family is yet to see what all the fuss is about, Mum's met her, why can't we?"

"Mum hasn't met her, she's seen where she lives, that's all and, actually, you may get to meet her tonight," Eric told his brother. "I'm taking her to the Old Bell for a couple of drinks and I may bring her back here afterwards, so if you want to see what the fuss is about, make sure you're home this evening."

"Count me in," Robert said as he grabbed a slice of toast and made his way out the door. "See you tonight little brother."

*****

The evening passed and both Eric and Yvonne were sharing stories and getting to know each other. Eric got to realise that in actual fact, Yvonne was nothing like the cold exterior she projected and, when she opened up, her heart was as beautiful as she looked. It was when Yvonne looked slightly tired of Eric's jokes that he asked if she would like to walk over to his house and meet some of his family.

"I know they're eager to meet you, I've told them a lot about you," Eric encouraged.

"Good things I hope," Yvonne answered rhetorically. "Go on then, why not."

Eric said goodnight to some of his friends who were in the pub having a quiet drink and then made his way outside, holding the door open for his date and offering her his jacket.

"Thank you," she replied, nestling her way underneath the shield of his smart tailored jacket.

They stopped outside number 106 and Eric pulled Yvonne back by her hand.

"Please be warned, my family love a joke and are sure not to hold back on your account. If and when you want to leave, give me the nod, OK? Otherwise we'll make a move in about an hour so to get you home before your curfew."

"My curfew!" Yvonne exclaimed. "You cheeky devil, it's not a curfew, just the time my father likes me home," she said indignantly.

"Yes, a curfew," Eric said under his breath, and received a slap on the arm in return.

They made their way inside and Eric could hear that his nan was home upstairs.

"Mum? Dad?" Eric called.

"In here, dear," Ellen replied, calling out from the lounge in front of them.

Oddly the door was shut but Eric opened it, and welcomed Yvonne inside. Ellen, Richard and Robert were all in, playing what looked like a game of cards.

"You must be Yvonne?" Ellen asked as she stood from her chair. "It's a pleasure to finally meet you," she said as she wrapped her arms around Yvonne.

"Poker, Yvonne?" Richard asked as he stood to greet his son's date.

"Not for me, thank you, but I would like to watch you play," Yvonne replied.

"You most certainly won't," Ellen said. "Come, we can stop play for ten minutes. Yvonne, what can I get you to drink?".

"I'd love a black coffee if that's OK?"

"Perfect," Ellen replied as she made her way into the kitchen.

"So you're the girl I've heard all about. Wow! I can see why," Robert said as he greeted his brother's date with a wink and a cheeky grin.

Yvonne sat down and seemed to be enjoying getting to know all of Eric's family. Robert didn't stay long and told his parents that he'd kick their arses some other time and headed out with friends. Ellen had busied herself in the kitchen cleaning plates and cups from the evening's dinner and Eric excused himself whilst he visited the toilet, which left Yvonne alone with Richard. They'd got into a discussion about her time studying to be a secretary at Pitman's College when he cut her off mid-sentence.

"Come on boy. You come to see me? Oh, come here you pretty boy." He said gesturing towards the empty doorway in front of him. "Oh, you're such a good boy." He said as he fell back into the chair besides Yvonne.

Needless to say, Yvonne kept her distance from her date's father as she watched him, thinking he must be mad. Whilst Yvonne longed for Eric to re-enter the room, Richard meanwhile, continued his antics.

"You think I'm crazy don't you?" he asked.

"Well…." Yvonne started to reply.

"You don't need to be polite, I would in your shoes but look at the hairs on my arms, and on the back of my neck,"

Richard said as he gestured with his arms towards her and lowered his head for her to inspect his neck.

Yvonne was dubious as she did as she was told but agreed that every hair was stood entirely on end.

"Do you notice it's suddenly cold in here?" He didn't wait for her reply. "The temperature's dropped because we're not alone. My old dog, Prince, has come to see me. He does sometimes. He died two years ago but that doesn't stop him coming to see his old master from time to time," he said as he continued to scratch and stroke thin air.

Yvonne sat speechless and sighed with relief as Eric walked back into the room.

"I think it's time I took you home," Eric said and Yvonne didn't bat an eyelid at the prospect.

During the fifteen minute journey, Yvonne was a little quieter than usual and Eric suspected what may have happened.

"My Dad's done something, hasn't he?" he asked. "What did he do?"

Yvonne sat quiet for a moment. "Prince?" she said slowly, wondering if it would trigger something that Eric may know.

He smiled. "So he told you about Prince?" Yvonne nodded. "Can I assume Prince came to see him tonight?" Again, she nodded.

It was hard for Eric to explain about his father in ten minutes but he gave it a go and without much persuasion, Yvonne had agreed to sit in on one of Richard's Ouija boards the following week.

Great, Eric thought. I really liked this one.

*****

It was Thursday, June 17th 1964 and, as usual at Richard's meetings, people arrived on time and everyone was ready and waiting, including Yvonne. She'd never thought much about life after death; her parents, although Christians, didn't believe in ghosts or the paranormal, to them it was all nonsense and so Yvonne had been bought up to believe the same. However, she was curious. She'd told her parents that she was going over to Eric's house and being cooked a meal by Ellen, which was a slight twist on the truth. She had shared a delicious meal of sausage casserole which had been cooked by Ellen, and they'd talked briefly about the events that may or may not unfold that evening.

Whilst the women washed the dirty dishes, Ellen explained, "It doesn't always work. It's not through want of trying, it's just that sometimes the ghosts don't want to speak."

"Doesn't it frighten you to think of what's going on upstairs?" Yvonne asked, trying to make sense of the situation.

"Richard knows what he's doing and I trust that. It's something that goes a long way into his past, and of which I have been aware since the beginning of our relationship. It's not something I get involved in but that's not to say that it hasn't involved me in the past."

Yvonne found it hard to believe that Ellen could show such lack of concern in what her husband was doing but she chose not to ask too many questions. She didn't even know whether or not she believed in it yet.

Ten people turned up for the meeting that night, Eric, Yvonne and Richard included. The guests stood in the room upstairs, as Richard entered with a large wooden board. It was an inch or so thick and Yvonne could see that it had writing on one side. The other side was bare.

"OK, for those of you new to this, this is a Ouija board. It's a medium that I use to speak to the dead. As most of you are aware, I will place a planchette in the centre of the board and when we feel that we have a presence in the room with us, I will ask the spirit questions; it will then move the planchette to spell out its answer. Does that make sense?" Richard looked directly at Yvonne, who nodded in agreement. "Then let's begin."

Everyone placed their fingertips on the wooden planchette and Yvonne followed suit. She didn't know really what she was doing or what to expect but she was eager to learn. Having never experienced anything untoward before now, she had no reason to be nervous, so she wasn't. When Richard begun asking questions, Yvonne found herself stifling a giggle. Perhaps it was the nerves, she didn't know, but she felt her cheeks turn red and her shoulders begin to shake as a grin covered her face.

"Is something funny?" Richard asked.

"Of course not," Yvonne answered, still desperately trying not to laugh.

"If you think this is funny, I'd like for you to try this on your own with James, as James is also a non-believer."

James Petterson was a young man who lived in London, not far from Liverpool Street, and was put in touch with Richard's evenings through a friend of John's. He didn't believe in ghosts but had lost his mother a couple of months before and was eager to try to contact her, if that were possible.

As directed, everyone removed their finger besides Yvonne and James as Richard continued to call out the questions.

"If anyone's there, give me a sign. If anyone's there, give me a sign. Tell me your name," he asked.

Yvonne sat still for a moment, catching James' eye every so often but neither one of them wanted to draw any more attention to the situation than the other. Yvonne no longer wanted to laugh as she now had several pairs of eyes on her, including Eric who she knew would be embarrassed if she made a scene; so she sat still and waited for something, or nothing, to happen. Within a minute or two, the planchette began to move. First of all it just flickered, moving only a centimetre or two, but then it started to circle the board.

Yvonne immediately looked at James. She knew that he was the one who must be making the piece move.

"Is that you? You're doing that," she insisted as she felt the smooth movement of the wooden piece swirling around the board beneath her index finger.

"It's not me, I swear. I thought it was you moving it," James proclaimed as he sat watching the piece move faster and faster beneath his touch.

Both of them sat watching it move, unable to comprehend what was happening or how. Yvonne could feel the wood burn beneath her finger and the way it glided across the table wasn't the way it would feel if someone was pushing it; it was darting about in every direction and moving too fast to have been pushed if James had been the culprit. It was clear that something else was in the room with them. Then it stopped moving.

"J," Richard said.

The glass moved again, this time a fast smooth motion that took a fraction of a second to come to a stop.

"A," he continued.

And again it moved.

"C. K. I. E. Jackie."

Yvonne realised that the board had spelt out the name Jackie and when she looked at James' face, it was evident he was as clueless as she was.

"Please stop," Yvonne cried. "I don't want to continue. Please do whatever you need to do and let me go downstairs with Ellen. Sorry, Eric," she turned and dropped her head down, "I don't want anything to do with this."

And so Richard asked Jackie to leave and said the Lord's Prayer before letting Yvonne leave the room and join Ellen downstairs. Although nothing awful or disastrous happened that night, it was enough to warn Yvonne off for good. It would be a long time before she delved into anything like that again and it wasn't something she intended to tell her parents about either. She would choose to retire after dinner from now on.

Chapter Twenty

Yvonne and Eric continued dating through the summer and into the winter of 1964 and before they knew it, another year had passed. Although still intrigued, Yvonne never involved herself again in one of Richard's spiritual evenings and never felt the same about the house. Whenever she visited number 106, whether it was for dinner or just passing through, she'd never let Eric out of her sight. Even when she needed the toilet, she'd have Eric sit outside the door, playing on his guitar so that she knew she wasn't alone. What happened upstairs in the front lounge had changed her perception on life, and death, and she didn't want to tempt fate or the unknown by playing around with it.

1965 turned into an exciting year for the Camps. Eric traded in his motorbike for a stunning, dark green Morris Oxford, mainly to impress Yvonne and which succeeded in doing, and in the same moment proposed to her and she said "yes". Yvonne had slotted in perfectly with the Camp family and they welcomed her with open arms. She had become particularly close to Flo after Henry passed away and, just as the rest of the family were, she was devastated to hear the news that Flo had developed what would now be recognised as Alzheimer's Disease. It came as a surprise to the whole family and particularly to Flo who was still in pieces about the loss of her husband. Flo had always been such an independent woman, always worked hard to support her family, so a disease like Alzheimer's came as a huge shock. After losing Henry, she spent her days gardening or making suppers for the family and in the afternoons she loved nothing more than getting her secret stash of sweets out and throwing them to passing schoolchildren. They all loved her.

The same year, Robert left home to live with Janet, leaving Keith the only one settled still at number 106. Keith was nineteen years old now. He had a girlfriend, Jean, whom he liked a lot and was the first relationship he considered to be serious. Keith was pretty relaxed and didn't take anything too seriously. Many people who'd experienced the level of menacing paranormal encounters that Keith had would have wanted to get as far away from the house as possible, but Keith was never frightened by what he saw; in a way it intrigued him as it did his father. He didn't share the same passion for communicating with the dead, but neither did he run from the experiences he'd had.

Keith worked as a mechanic and sometimes found himself at home during the day when everyone else, besides Flo, was either out at work or busying themselves with chores. On October 18th 1965, Keith was able to finish his work in the morning and by two o'clock, had packed up and gone home. He often caught the bus as the journey took less than fifteen minutes, but he decided to walk that particular day as it was unusually warm for October, the sun sat high in the sky and he thought it was probably going to be the last time in months that he'd be able to leave his coat off and enjoy the walk. He made it home just before three o'clock and as usual, no one was home besides his Nan, who was happily looking out of the window upstairs, waiting for the schoolchildren to walk by.

"Hi, Nan," he called out without waiting for a reply.

He made his way through the lounge and into the kitchen to make himself a sandwich. He found some bread in the tin which was on its last legs, buttered it and layered on some cheese and ham that was lying out in the fridge and made his way into the sitting room at the back of the house. He had some time to kill and decided to do absolutely nothing with it, sit back and relax. He cleaned his plate and put it down on the floor next to him, leant back into the soft chair and closed his eyes. He thought about his life and of his latest girlfriend, Jean and the plans for when he'd see her later that evening. As he felt himself drift into a dream-like state, there was a very sudden and almighty thud that came from the opposite end of the room. It sounded loud enough to be the collapse of an entire bookcase or someone trying to break their way through the solid wall between the sitting room and the kitchen.

"Hello?" he asked speculatively as he stood to his feet.

The sitting room was a moderate size but by no means large enough to hide a person in but he felt the need to investigate. As far as he could see, the room was empty. There was a small table and ornament cupboard at the opposite end, where the crash had come from, but everything looked in place and intact; there wasn't anything visible that could have caused the calamity.

He moved extremely slowly across the room, waiting for one of his brothers to jump out at him, or perhaps it was one of Yvonne's jokes, she had the kind of humour that would find it funny to scare the crap out of someone and then point her finger laughing. However, he knew that she was terrified of number 106 and the chances of her being brave enough to sit in an empty room by herself, waiting for her moment, was unlikely.

Keith straightened himself out as he realised he was crouching low to the ground, like a predator hunting his prey and, as he did, he suddenly saw a shuddering movement from behind the red Victorian chair that had its pride of place in the corner of the room in front of him. It was a figure crouched down low, low enough that Keith wasn't able to see its face. Was it one of his brothers? No, it was too small to be an adult, it must be a child.

"Hello?" he asked again as he reached about ten feet away from the enigma.

There was no reply but, as he drew closer, so the figure fidgeted and edged its way further into the corner behind the furniture. Even though Keith had plenty of experience of the paranormal, he never expected anything to happen. Every time something did, he would try to rationalise the situation first, and this was no exception. It hadn't occurred to him that the apparition he saw in front of him could be a ghost, it was only logical that it was a child, lost perhaps, unable to find his or her way home. This is quite possibly why, every time he did experience something paranormal, it would always shake him up so badly. Although expecting the least, as he made his way across the room, feeling sweat build up on the back of his neck and hands, his knees began to tremble and he could see that the perplexing figure's face was a vast contrast to the child he was imagining. The small manifestation resembled a goblin that you'd be likely to see in a computer game or fantasy film with dark, wrinkled, leathery skin; a long, pointed nose that matched the angle of its chin and dark, narrow eyes that were darting around the room at a speed Keith wasn't able to comprehend. And then, from behind him, as if announced on loudspeakers around the room, Keith heard a very deep, masculine voice;

"THAT MADE YOU JUMP."

He shot his body round like a dart to face the direction of where he thought he'd heard the voice and standing in front of him, on the same sofa he'd been resting on just minutes before, was a man no taller than three feet. His head crooked, face covered in sores and blisters, dressed in a dark grey suit, that made him look as though he was dressed for his morgue photograph.

Keith stood still, unable to move, paralysed to the spot, watching the eerie creature jump and laugh in front of him. Neither of them threatened the other, just observed, until he heard keys push into the front door's lock and his mother's voice call out;

"Anyone home?"

Keith turned to make his way to the door, not wanting his mum to witness the scene but when he found his feet and reached for the handle, he turned to see that the room behind him was empty of all things living, and dead.

*****

The house on Poultney Road said farewell to Eric when he married and bought a house with Yvonne, leaving just Keith behind, but not for long. Out of all three children, Keith was by far the most receptive and also the more willing and this continued right up until he left home at the age of twenty-one, in 1966 but the house wasn't going to let him leave without giving him a proper farewell. As was customary, Richard did his occasional séances and Ouija boards which although they were becoming a little more infrequent, still happened. It was early one Sunday evening in September 1966 and Keith was at home with Flo upstairs, making herself busy as usual whilst Ellen cooked dinner for when Richard returned home from the pub. It became a regular thing that he would go out for a few drinks on a Sunday afternoon with his friends whilst Ellen stayed at home and cooked a roast dinner for the family. Eric sometimes came home with Yvonne and Robert too, but on this particular day, she was cooking for the four of them.

Keith had been out the night before with friends at the Flamingo, a jazz club in Soho. It was one of his favourite ways to spend an evening and he liked nothing more than having a few drinks, listening to soul music and watching beautiful women around him enjoying themselves. He'd stayed late, until past five in the morning and had spent most of the following day in bed. Ellen left him alone in his bedroom, knowing that to wake him would cause no end of fuss. She'd put the roast potatoes in the oven with the meat and took ten minutes to have a break and put her feet up in the lounge. She'd poured herself a small tipple of port and laid back on the sofa. As she felt herself drifting to sleep, she felt as though she was no longer alone. She turned round in her seat to see who was there but the room was empty.

"Keith?" she asked but there was no reply.

Dismissing her senses, she laid back once again and closed her eyes. Feeling uneasy, she opened her eyes and gasped at what she saw in front of her. Projected on the wall above the fireplace was Keith's face staring down at her. She jumped to her feet in alarm, ran down the hall and stepped towards the door with every intention of checking on Keith in his bedroom.

"Keith, are you awake in there? she called out but his reply came from upstairs.

"Mum, I'm up here," he replied, from somewhere on the second floor of the house.

239

Ellen made her way along the hall and up the stairs.

"Where are you?" she asked.

"I'm in here," Keith's voice replied and it was coming from the back bedroom where her mother-in-law slept.

Ellen hesitated. The image she'd seen downstairs could have been a warning.

She slowly walked to the top of the stairs and made her way across the landing to the bedroom. As she got closer, she was able to hear Keith talking.

Who's he talking to? she thought.

Eager to find out, she marched across the landing and opened the door. As she did, the room fell silent.

"Keith?" she said as she looked around the room. "Where are you?"

There was no reply. The room was dark and the curtains were drawn so she made her way across the room to open them. The thick drapes that fell in front of her moved, as though someone was behind them. She stopped in her tracks. Her eyes traced the room, looking for something to protect herself with, but there was nothing. Whilst looking, she noticed a pair of dirty brown boots poking out from beneath the curtains. It was as if whoever was wearing them knew that they'd been caught and shuffled their way further out of sight. As the feet disappeared, she then heard heavy breathing coming from the same place.

"Keith, is that you?" she said as she took her final step forward, reaching out for the edge of the drape.

She counted in her head to three and yanked on the material. She felt clammy beneath her fingers and simultaneously she heard Keith screaming downstairs. Revealing an empty window, Ellen turned on her heel and made her way back along the landing and down the stairs. She burst into Keith's bedroom only to find him sound asleep in bed. Ellen breathed a sigh of relief but at the same time, dropped down to her knees and wept.

She didn't often show her emotions or dwell on her troubles. She never shared the extent of her grief when Henry had died, nor did she at the loss of their first pet, Prince. She never told Richard about any money worries she might have and said nothing of the fact that for the past five years she had been visited in her sleep by a man in black. She kept this to herself as she knew what horror it would bring to her husband. She knew that Richard saw a man in black the day that his best friend, Harry, had died when he was a boy and that he'd been visited by him a number of times since but even Richard had told Ellen that he was relieved that he no longer had to see him and that, obviously, he now rested somewhere on the other side. Ellen knew this wasn't the case. It seemed that around the time that Richard stopped being haunted by the dark presence, so her dreams began.

The dreams, or rather, nightmares, differed slightly but one thing remained persistent. The man in black would always have her trapped in 106 Poultney Road with no means of escape.

It always began with her waking from a nightmare in her bedroom. She'd feel for Richard in the bed next to her but he wasn't there. She'd reach for her side light but the switch didn't work. She'd try to call for Richard but no words would come out. Making her way out of bed, she scrambled her way across the black room and felt for the light switch only to find that the electricity was out completely. As she opened the bedroom door, he was always there, face-to-face with her. The man in black, the man her husband feared more than anything else; the man who had haunted her entire family for the past thirty years and, each time in her dream, she would try to get a better look at his features but she was never able to remember them when she woke up. Always able to push past him, she would run in every room, calling out for her husband and children, searching for Flo or anyone who could help her, but there was no one there. Always two paces behind her was the evil entity. All doors and windows were locked, with no access to the outside world. She would try to smash windows, punch walls, and the doors, but to no avail. She was trapped in the house alone and frightened in the company of something that she knew, deep down, wanted her dead. Besides her own erratic breathing, she was always woken by the sound of laughter, a deep, malevolent laughter. The one thing that worried Ellen more than anything was that whenever she would wake from these dreams, it would take at least a week for the bruising on her fists to go down, which were almost impossible to hide from her husband.

Chapter Twenty-One

The months soon turned to years and, before they knew it, Ellen and Richard were made grandparents. Robert had a child, Claire, with his wife Janet, and Eric and Yvonne had their first child, Jane, in 1970. Oddly enough, Eric and Yvonne moved into the house opposite number 106 and they spent many happy years there. It worked in their favour as as they had a full-time babysitter should they need one; Ellen was always on call. Over the years, Yvonne became particularly close to Richard, although she never again participated in one of his Ouija boards or séances; although she loved to listen to his stories and discuss the supernatural with him.

Richard continued to hold his meetings but they became fewer and further between. Whenever he did, he got plenty of interest, always from word of mouth. Between 1967 and 1977 he held around forty Ouija boards and séances and around seventy-five percent of them were successful in contacting the dead. He never felt too disappointed when he had a quiet night; he never put it down to anything personal, just sometimes the spirits of number 106 didn't feel sociable. No one ever paid to attend his evenings and they were always given first refusal on the next one so no-one ever left feeling disappointed.

Flo, or Lolly Nan, as everyone had come to know her, was more affected by Alzheimer's as the years passed but she continued to live at number 106. She would sit herself at the front window every single day, watching the world go by.

She'd often watch Yvonne walking to and from the station to travel to work each day and comment on how she looked to Ellen, as if she was some stranger living down the street.

"Just who does she think she is?" Flo would shout out to Ellen, "Dressed up to the nines wearing red lipstick and heels. She really thinks she's something doesn't she."

Ellen always laughed it off; Flo meant no harm and was in fact very close to Yvonne, who in 1975 had nursed her through shingles when no one else in the family would go near her.

With just three of them living in number 106, Flo upstairs by herself, Richard and Ellen living downstairs, they still witnessed paranormal activity around their home but were used to it. Regularly, both Richard and Ellen would be wakened in the night by someone calling out Robert's name. To begin with, they thought it must be Flo upstairs, but one time it happened when all three of them were together in the kitchen. Nothing ever came of this and Ellen would often say aloud by way of an answer;

"He doesn't live here anymore."

And it seemed to do the trick.

There had always been a strange, damp smell that was more evident in Keith's bedroom and at the top of the stairs, which seemed to get worse over the years. It became so bad in the end that Ellen would have to cover it with a spray each morning and evening, otherwise visitors would often complain.

The Camps always knew that the house was haunted and that they'd brought more traffic to it than had originally been there, but the one spirit which didn't belong to the house and instead chose to haunt Richard and his family, no matter where they lived, was the man in black. As Richard had grown older, he was visited by him less frequently and this pleased him; it was the one ghost that he didn't feel comfortable with and, although he'd been the one who'd awakened his initial interest in the paranormal, he was also the one that terrified him.

*****

In the late Spring of 1977, Richard had organised a meeting for eight o'clock one Thursday evening. For one reason or another, only four people showed up; Mable, Phyllis, Bessie and their niece, Diane Marple. Diane was eighteen years old and the youngest person to sit in on one of his evenings. She was a young woman with long blonde hair, naturally beautiful with features of a Disney Princess with huge blue eyes. Richard had been dubious about letting her participate because of her age but she'd heard about him through her father and, since losing her mother to a devastating case of breast cancer, she'd begged Richard to let her attend in hope that she may be connected to her mother.

Richard chose to do a Ouija board as they seemed to work better with fewer participants. He'd already explained to Diane that the possibilities of contacting her mother were down to utter chance and that he couldn't make any promises, but she agreed to take part and accept whatever unfolded during the evening. However, she hadn't quite prepared herself for the events ahead of her. Not even Richard was ready for what was in store.

Everyone arrived on time and waited upstairs for Richard to join them. As Flo was unwell, she remained downstairs with Ellen throughout the duration of the Ouija board; they couldn't risk her walking in and interrupting a session. Richard brought into the room a new, varnished, dark wood board that had the letters of the alphabet and numbers burnt into the wood as well as a very distinct GOOD BYE that had been engraved in the bottom right hand corner. He'd made the board himself and was excited to be using it for the first time.

"So, tonight we welcome Diane who is joining us for the first time." He spoke to the rest of the group whilst gesturing at the young guest standing over the other side of the table from him. "This will be her first Ouija board but she has reason to be here and is excited about getting started."

Diane smiled at Richard as she remembered her mother's sweet face, which had changed dramatically over the last few months as her bones became frail and skin turned grey. She had always been so close to her mother that she was convinced she'd visit her during the session.

Richard ran through the necessaries before concluding with a warning to everyone not to let go of the glass.

"As some of you know, one of the most important things to remember during a séance or Ouija board is never to break the chain. By doing so you are offering whatever it is you have connected with a free ride into our world, and once you do, there's no turning back. So no matter what happens or what you may see or hear, you do not break contact with this planchette. Once we have wished farewell to the spirit or spirits, I will then tell you that it is safe to let go."

Richard had refrained from using a glass when one smashed during contact with a playful spirit a few years previously. It was also harder for people to fake a connection using a planchette compared with a glass.

"Understood?" he asked.

"Understood," his guests replied in unison.

As they did, the bedroom light smashed above their heads as though someone had thrown something at it. The glass fell and covered the solid pine table that they were standing around, oddly not a single shard had rested on the board.

"It looks as though we have company waiting for us tonight," Richard muttered.

He looked up and caught sight of Diane, who had horror plastered all over her face.

"Everyone OK and ready to proceed?" he asked, to ensure Diane hadn't changed her mind, but everyone sat still and nodded. "Then let's begin. If anyone's there, please give us a sign; if anyone's there, please give us a sign."

As always, Richard's guests repeated his words, each one of them eager to see something; to have that reassurance that life does continue after death.

Richard stopped talking. He stood completely motionless as he felt every single hair on his body stand on end. The temperature in the room dropped in a matter of seconds as he felt someone, or something, stroking the back of his neck. The touch was freezing, as if the fingertips were coated in ice but as they moved up and along his hair-line, they left a burning trail behind them.

The planchette moved. It was so quick that they almost missed the first spelling. R. They all spoke the letter aloud. I. And again. C.H.A.R.D

"Richard, they're speaking to you," Bessie said.

"Who's this? Who are we speaking to?" Richard asked, a little more demanding than he anticipated.

The planchette moved again and, as it did, Diane screamed in pain.

"Mum," she yelled, "please stop! Please don't hurt my mother," she implored whilst looking to the right corner of the room behind where Richard was standing.

"Diane, look away, you must concentrate on the board," Richard insisted as he turned to face her point of focus.

"But I can see her, she's trying to get away," Diane screamed. "He's going to kill her."

"Who is with your mother Diane? Whoever it is can't kill her, she's already dead." As he said those harsh words, so the young girl in front of him broke down in tears.

"Please, spirit, tell us your name," intoned Richard as the bedroom window smashed in front of him.

The planchette moved once again, quicker and more sharply than would be possible of a human action.

T.H.E.M.A.N.I.N.B.L.A.C.K

"The man in black. So you've waited all this time to speak to me. What is it you have to say?" Richard shouted.

"Who is he?" Diane begged. "Will he cause us harm Richard?"

And then there was nothing. Even the bitterly cold wind that was blowing in through the window stopped. The air was still; not a sound to be heard.

The quiet before the storm.

"What do you want from me?" Richard asked.

E.L.L.E.N the board spelled, and before Richard could respond he heard the screeching of his wife from downstairs. Her screams so fierce, so petrified, that he forgot to follow his own protocol in his fear; the essential steps he'd always warned his guests about for the thirty years he'd been doing the Ouija boards. He didn't end the session. He broke the chain and literally threw himself out of the door and onto the landing. Every step felt like a mile, the stairs steeper than he remembered as he jumped his way down them.

"Ellen where are you?" he screamed as he raced into the front room which was empty.

His wife's screams became more and more traumatised.

"Richard, help me," Ellen cried.

Silence. Richard stood in the middle of the hallway with only the sound of the ticking clock for comfort, which echoed around him. He felt as though he was dreaming.

"Ellen? Mum?" he called, but there was no answer.

The house was in pitch black. When the bulb smashed upstairs, the electricity in the entire house must have blown. He couldn't even hear his guests upstairs. The house felt empty. As he made his way along the hallway and further into the house, the atmosphere grew in density like

252

something had vacuumed the oxygen around him. He rubbed his eyes in hope that his vision would be clearer and the haze would lift but it didn't. He was certain that his wife would be in the sitting room in front of the kitchen where he'd left her, and his mother, earlier that evening but as he stepped past his bedroom door, he heard a floorboard creak from inside.

"Ellen?" he asked again.

There was no reply and so put his hand on the metal door knob which burnt its way through his flesh. Instinct pulled his palm away, leaving behind the top layer of skin. Undeterred by the pain, Richard grabbed hold of the knob again, turned it as fast as he could and pushed open the door. It opened with ease and as it did, it revealed, lying in the bed in front of him - the same bed that he shared with his wife - the two most important women in his life; Ellen and his mother, Flo. Neither one of them was moving and neither one looked conscious.

It was at that point that he saw him.

He stood about six feet high and was dressed from head to foot in black. Unlike the grim reaper, Richard was able to now see this man's face. Richard's mind questioned for a moment whether this entity standing in front of him may be something demonic but, as he took a step closer, he was able to make out a face that, although not dissimilar to a human face it was terrifying all the same. Jet black eyes that sat deep within their sockets; a slightly crooked nose that ended in a point but, as far as Richard could see, he didn't have nostrils and his mouth had no lips. As Richard stared into the eyes of the entity before him it grimaced, showing his tiny, yellowed stained teeth that looked like small feline fangs. As its face smiled, so the skin cracked around its eyes, making them sink deeper into the flesh creating hollow edges around its eyeballs. The creature turned to face the bed.

"Please. Tell me what it is you want. Why have you been following me for so many years? What do you want from me?" Richard pleaded and, as he did, he took another step towards the evil presence that stood before him.

"It's not you I want, Richard." As the spectre spoke, so the room filled with a putrid stench of vomit. "It has always been Ellen. Tell her I'll be waiting for her."

And, as if he'd never been there, the man in black dropped through the floor. No puddle, no cloud of smoke, nothing; completely vanished. Richard froze momentarily, but the stirring of his wife bought him to his senses. He rushed the final few paces to her side, lifted her into his arms and wrapped them around her.

"Ellen, are you OK? What happened, do you remember anything?" he asked, wiping the tears from his cheek.

"The last thing I remember was dozing off and then feeling as though I was choking," Ellen explained. "How did we end up here? Flo?" she said turning to look at her mother-in-law lying in the bed beside her. "Are you OK? Richard, what happened?"

Richard reached out for his mother's hand and held on to them both for some time. He didn't say a word more to them that night, not to his family nor to his guests, who seemed to be in a trance-like state when he went back upstairs. From that night on, Richard didn't touch a Ouija board or séance again. He tried not to think about what had happened that night, and wanted desperately to believe it never did. It was the only way he felt that he could protect his wife from an evil that was so deadly earnest in its intent that it made him sick to his stomach.

It wasn't until he was on his deathbed six years later, that he told his wife, Ellen, what had happened on that April night at 106 Poultney Road and he made her promise that she would never encourage spirits again. He made his children all make the same promise to him before he passed away of lung cancer, as the most terrifying thing had happened to him that night. He wasn't possessed or almost killed; he didn't have an out of body experience; far worse, he was made a promise by something or someone that had terrified him his entire life and already taken his best friend from him all those years ago. That night, the man in black threatened to wait for his wife Ellen and what terrified Richard the most was the implication that he meant that he would wait for her on the other side.

However, what the man in black may not have realised was that Richard would be waiting too.

Chapter Twenty-two

About a month before my granddad died in December 1982, he and my mother, Yvonne, got chatting one evening after dinner. They were talking about the future and what it had in store; about my granddad's life growing up, what he missed and the things he'd never got round to doing. He made two promises to my mother. One was that if there was such a thing as life after death, he would prove it to her. He didn't know how but, somehow, he would. Secondly, if reincarnation was possible, he would come back as one of her animals. Being an animal lover himself and knowing what a kind-hearted woman my mother was, especially with her animals, he would want to come back reincarnated as one of her pets.

The week before his cremation, Richard's body was laid in the chapel of rest and Yvonne went to visit him. Eric was meant to go with her but something at work had cropped up and he wasn't able to get away from the office. The children already had their sitter, Sharon, who was also their next-door neighbour, so Yvonne had an hour spare and decided to pay her last respects. She arrived at the chapel shortly after four o'clock on 12th December 1982, parked her car and made her way inside, out of the bitterly cold wind that blew through the bare branches around the graves outside. When she had visited other family members previously, the priest had been present and so she imagined it to be the same this time but, as she entered the large chapel, there was no one to be seen.

"Hello?" she called.

Her call was unreturned and echoed around the hollow space, sounding like a thousand voices calling out to her. She could see the open casket that Richard was lying in at the back of the room. A little nervous, she made her way over to him, her thin, stiletto heels clinking with every step against the marble floor, sounding like a million raindrops hitting the ground around her. As she approached the side of the coffin, she took a deep breath, not really knowing what he was going to look like now that the blood had drained, and with it all of his emotions and memories, taken to another place. But as she caught sight of him, she felt at ease. He looked the same, slim face, pale skin and dressed in a dapper navy suit, white shirt and matching tie.

"Oh, Richard, you really will be missed. Who will tell me stories to stop me sleeping at night now?" she said wryly as a smile grew on her lips and a tear fell from her water-filled eyes.

As she reached forward to kiss his stone-cold cheek, she heard what sounded like a breath and, as she did, Richard's chest rose from its motionless state and appeared to inhale.

"Richard?" Yvonne said as she stepped back in astonishment. "Richard, is that you?" she asked, but before she knew it the air seemed to be released from his lungs and his body returned to its stationary position.

Yvonne still managed to briefly kiss Richard on the cheek before making a swift exit.

When she was back in her car, her body relaxed and her mind traced what she had just experienced when she suddenly remembered the promise that Richard had made to her a month or so earlier. Was that Richard's last chance of proving life carries on before he was able to rest in peace, or perhaps his last chance before he came back as one of Yvonne's pets, or children?

In April 1983, Yvonne was thirty-seven years old with two children, one twelve, the other nine; a dog and a cat. Her life was complete. One morning she woke up early and felt particularly sick, dashed to the toilet and vomited twice. She put it down to something she must have eaten, until it happened on the next two consecutive mornings. Thinking it was impossible at her age especially when the difficulties she'd had after giving birth to her second child had meant, according to the doctors, that she wouldn't be able to have children again, she left off doing a pregnancy test for two weeks. On the second week she took a test, waited two minutes and saw a second line pop up in front of her. Against all odds, she was pregnant.

Yvonne gave birth to me on 7th October 1983, ten months after my granddad had died. Coincidence? It could be, but the months that followed my birth made it very believable that I had a lot in common with my granddad, a man I had never met.

As I said at the beginning of this book, I haven't written the story to scare you, nor has it been written with a gruesome ending or with horrific murders along the way, because that's not how I believe the supernatural works. My granddad wasn't ever trying to be a medium, he never tried to contact ghosts that only he could see, he shared his gift with others and the experiences that my family had were all shared and witnessed by guests at his meetings, or with each other.

As a family, we only ever had one piece of hard evidence of the paranormal and that was the photograph that was taken during one of my granddad's séances of my nanny Ellen covered in tiny babies. She kept it until she died but, after going through all of her belongings and photographs, it was never found.

Do I believe in ghosts? Of course. Do I believe that something else exists besides what we see and feel? Most definitely. Do I wish I'd met my granddad and learnt first-hand what it's like to witness such phenomena? I didn't need to because my granddad's ability passed onto me. I didn't ask for it, and from the moment I was born it was evident that something followed me, and that I had a gift. I never looked for it; it found me.

Artist's impression of the house. (Claire Hughes)